Thug and Harmony

by Resa and Jroc

To receive future updates from Shani Greene-Dowdell Presents, text Nayberry to 22828.

CHAPTER 1
THUG

Bankhead, Atlanta, GA

I pulled up to Gator's crib bumping that Kevin Gates "2 Phones" shit, "Trap jumping like ring, ring, ring." The bass from my 15-inch subs thumped in my trunk as the car came to a stop. I had waited around 'til a little after ten o'clock to give that nigga time to get up. When I saw him sitting on the porch playing dominos, I knew it was all good.

Gator was one of those motherfuckers who could act bipolar at times. One day he would be all cool and shit, but the next he would be dressed up saying he was going to handle business or something, whatever that meant. He never did say where he was going. For all I knew, the nigga could have been going to church or some shit and just didn't want me to know, but that was his business... I just noticed the change.

It had been a minute since I'd been over to Gator's crib, mainly because for the last seven months, I was locked up in the Fulton County jail; that meant no weed, no pussy, and worst of all no motherfucking money.

I killed the engine and grabbed the rillo from the console. It was hard as fuck to stay out the game; fast money is like an addiction. I been hustling all my life, since I was like fifteen so that shit's in my blood. After being released for only two days, my inner soul was screaming for the block scene. Even though I had sixty-seven bands stashed away, a nigga needed to get straight back on the grind just to keep from falling off. Having cash is one thing, but keeping it is another. I would need to spend as little as I could, and that meant

3

sleeping from crib to crib and eating at my sister's. Being away from the block for seven months was a long time for a nigga who was used to getting money on the daily and I just couldn't let a minute slip by without trying to get this paper. Police say they lost my phone, so that shit was another fucking loss. Most of my clientele was gone and I was going to have to start letting niggas know I had touched back down. That's why I wasted no time coming over to Gator's and getting right back on my grizzy.

"Got damn, Thug. Is my eyes playing tricks on me, my neezy?"

Of course that nigga knew it was me, ain't no other nigga out this way gripping a yellow eighty-four box Chevy with the bacon soda logo painted on it. I could have gotten a Benz or something, but on the real ion really dig that new car shit. I like ole schools, hard body with big rims. No matter how much paper a nigga was getting, I still was gone keep it gangster; it was always ole school or nothing.

"What it be like blood?"

"Shid, holding the block down like a nigga in Afghanistan. What it is my nigga?" Gator said as we shook secretly and curved our fingers making that infamous letter. There was a choppa lying on the side of him, on top of a wooden stool. Gator was in the middle of a game of dominos and sipping a brew. I picked up the choppa so I could sit down.

"Shid, ready to get back to this paper. You posted for the jack boys, huh?" Gator sold mid and loud.

"Hell, yeah. Put it in the air, my nigga. I see you got the rillo," he said taking a sip. Gator held the brew with one hand and glared greedily. I always knew there was something grimy behind those eyes.

"Bouta roll up now," I said taking a seat on the stool beside him and reached into my pocket. I took out a bag and dumped the weed into my lap before I turned to look up at him. "Aye, you get the rest of my bud when twelve pulled up?"

Seven months ago, me and Gator had so much trap that we couldn't stop the traffic from coming in. We were seeing ten G's a week easy until one day, twelve had pulled up on us and did a random shake down. I had stuffed a few ounces in my draws and that's what they caught me with, but I left a whole pound in a brown grocery bag in a brick beside the porch.

Gator's eyes dimmed slowly. "Hell, naw. Ain seen yo' weed, nigga," he said and placed the beer back to his lips. Me and Gator had pulled a lot of quick juugs together, so I knew when he was lying.

"Bruh, gone with that bullshit and don't be getting all brick with yo' tone either. I just asked yo' ass. Shid, nigga, put it on some."

"Bruh, on the real, ain seen no motherfucking weed around here, damn. Nigga, if I had found some weed lying around this bitch, I would have sold it or smoked that shit up."

I wiped my chin and just stared at that nigga for a second. Gator could be a grimy motherfucker and, even though he might have been my nigga, it was codes to the shit. I may have to just charge this one to the game, but if I ever found out he was lying to me, I would definitely get some straightening.

"Nah the fuck you wouldn't have nigga. Make me go up top on yo' ass," I said and, for a moment, everything got quiet. "Don't wor bout' it. I'm fina bounce back." I broke the gar down the middle and filled it with weed. It was a good thing I'd brought some money with me. Sometimes you just had to take a loss and re-up from a nigga even if you didn't want to. "I need to re-up then, my nigga. Let me get a pound," I said as I sealed the blunt and licked it. A little bit of tobacco got on my lip so I spat on the ground and waited until Gator got up to count up the money. Homie or not, ain need dat nigga knowing what the fuck I had in my pocket. "Gone head, nigga, I got the bread," I said holding the blunt with one hand and

5

gazing at him real sleekly.

"Ain got a pound, my nigga."

"Damn, Gator man. Fuck! Well, let me just get a half a pound."

He shook his head. "Bruh, ain got that either."

"Quarter pound?" I asked with a slow arch in my brows.

"You need some sandwich bags too?"

"Yeah, nigga, don't weed go in bags? Damn you smart as fuck."

"Look, nigga, just 'cause you been to jail don't mean you motherfucking Boosie now."

Gator went inside and I dug into my jeans, counted out what I needed, and put the rest back in my pocket. As he was getting it, I heard someone singing some R&B shit that sounded horrible as fuck. I shook my head and lit the blunt.

"Here, nigga." He came back outside, handed me an elbow of weed that had been broken off the corner of the pound.

"Hell, naw, nigga. Put that shit on the scale, Gator," I said looking the other way on his ass and took a long pull of weed into my lungs. As it came through my nose, I paid him a ruthless glare. Ion play that slick shit, especially when it comes to my paper. A nigga had just gotten out of jail and I ain need to be taking no shorts from no one.

"Man, got damn. Now I gotta go back in there and get the shit out the bathroom cabinet. Bree in there. You gone have to wait a minute," he said and took a seat. "You lucky. That's all I had left. Nigga, I gotta re-up today, too." Gator placed the sandwich bags on the table beside the dominos.

"Dayum… Shit jumping like dat?" I passed him the blunt and held up the bag. I'd missed out on all that paper. It looked like that fire. Gator usually had that good shit, so I knew it was, and the way he said shit had been popping, I could get off this pack real quick.

"Hell, yeah. I can't even serve these niggas until I make a move." Just as he said that shit, his phone rang and the screen door opened.

"Boy, you just don't give a fuck, do you? Yo ass just got out and you already trying to sell weed. Ain no pussy up in jail, nigga, you need to be trying to stay out." Gator slid in the door behind Bree. She liked me and I always knew that shit cause every time I came over, she would make it her business to come up in my face with that sly-way flirt shit, but she was Gator's little sister, so that shit was dead; it wasn't happening.

"Man, take yo li'l thirsty ass back inside." I looked the other way on her ass and smoked the rest of my blunt. Gator came back out and Bree took her little fast ass back in the house. Gator threw the bag of weed on the scale and it weighed perfectly, just a little bit over. "Well, nigga, you mays well let me have that shake too. I'll sell all that shit."

It wasn't much, only a few loose leaves in the bottom of the bag. Gator looked at me hard and long. A nigga don't wanna give yo ass shit for free and this was one of those times.

"Only cause yo' ass just got outta jail, nigga. The way shit going, I may end up needing you too, so Imma look out for you this time, but, Thug, don't try that shit no moe," he said as he took the money, counted it, and placed a rubber band around it. Just as he did so, his celly rang again. "What's the play? Who dis, Greg? Oh word shid," he paused and squeezed the bridge of his nose with the tips of his fingers.

Gator let out restless sigh, glanced at me once, and then continued his convo. "Bruh, ain even got no ounce. A nigga just came through got the last," Gator said and I waved at him quickly trying to get his attention. He took a long look at me. "Oh hold up, my nigga said he ah sell you an ounce of his shit," he said into the

7

phone and his mouth froze open then started back talking. "Yeah, shit fire, shid. It's the same shit I had. He right here. Imma send him to you right now." Gator hung up the phone and slid it into his front pocket. "Aye my nigga, Imma let you serve this nigga this once, but don't be tryna take my clientele," he said.

"Ah nigga, that's wassup. I need this paper." Full of excitement, my tone rose a notch as I stood up and broke down some weed and threw it on the scale until it weighed twenty-eight grams. "Aye my nigga, good looking for real." I tied the top, slid it into my pocket, and got the directions from Gator.

"Parkside Elementary. Don't go up in there asking for the nigga, just sit in the car and wait... He'll come out." Gator looked at me seriously. I could tell it really made him feel some type of way by letting me get that money.

Even though I was still on probation, I just couldn't let this money get away, so I jumped in my whip and turned up that Gates... shid, a nigga had some mu'fuckan money to go get.

***

I pulled up to the school and waited for this nigga named Greg to come outside. Gator wouldn't give me his number, so I had no way of knowing just when he would walk out those doors. I was waiting on an older dude to walk out wearing a janitor's uniform.

There were several nice cars in the parking lot. On my left was a small Jetta and on my right a Honda Civic Coupe, but there was no one out there except for me. I had my windows down. The ounce of weed was lying on the passenger seat. I had the mixtape playing in the deck so I was cool.

Ten more minutes had gone by and I heard a bell ring. Children ran through the halls and I could see a few teachers walking by and then the bell rang again and everything settled again. There was a police officer standing by the main doors. He opened it once to look out and then closed it. A few seconds later, the door opened again, but this time a woman came out. She was wearing a cream-colored blouse and a red skirt that curved around a set of hips that was banging. Reminded me of Gina from *Martin*. I could hear her heels tapping on the concrete as she walked. When I noticed she hadn't veered away from my direction, I lit a cigarette and bobbed my head to the music.

Bitch aint fina stop my money.

She walked towards the car that was parked to my right and I heard the doors unlock as she approached. As I looked that way, the plumes of smoke ran through my nose and by then the chick had made it to the driver side of the car beside me, but the motherfucker didn't get into her car. Instead, she looked down at the weed that was lying on my seat.

She pulled down her glasses with the tip of her finger and motioned with her head. "Excuse me, but is that what I think it is?"

"What's it to you? Shit, don't be worried 'bout what's up in my motherfucking car." On the real though, she was one fine ass motherfucking bitch though. Her nails and shit was done and she had on some cute ass makeup. I finally noticed the name tag hanging from the strap around her neck, Ms. Fletcher, but that didn't mean I was gone let her ass get all up in my business.

"Ahh," she said, pausing as she looked back at the building, but I didn't even trip. By the time the police got out here, I would be long gone. The last thing I needed was to catch a case on school ground. I was sure Greg was coming out soon, so I would wait a few more minutes after I shook this nosey ass bitch.

Finally, her gaze came back to me. She pointed at the weed then looked around again to see if anyone was looking her way. I didn't see the cop yet and there was no one coming out of the school, so I wasn't budging. She looked back at me and her eyes

9

dimmed a little as she pressed her lips together. "How much?" She bit her bottom lip greedily and looked at me with sharp and unfeeling eyes. For a minute, I thought about her trying to snitch and then I got caught up in the way her lips smoothed over the other one.

Damn! This caramelized dip looked sexy as fuck. Taking a second look, I noticed her ocean colored eyes. I had never seen a sista with no blue eyes in my life. *I'll eat dat pussy from da back and then throw some D's on it*, I said to myself, thinking of how I'd nut off in that pussy if I fucked it. I quickly brushed those thoughts away and thought more logical about the situation, wondering if I should just tell her how much the weed was or ask for her number instead.

Where in da hell did those blue eyes come from on a black woman? I became lost for a sec as a web of desire suddenly swept over me from outta nowhere.

"Ahem, are you going to answer my question anytime today? I don't have all day," she snapped with her brows furrowed. I looked deeper into her eyes and checked her demeanor. She seemed satisfied when she saw no one was paying her any mind but, on the real, I still wasn't quite convinced.

"Whatchu asking all them got damn questions for? Is you working for the man? Shid, what? You trying to cop some weed or something? What the play is, shawty?"

"Because I want to purchase it from you. That is why you're here, right?" Ms. Fletcher asked with an arch finally settling on her right brow. "I know you're looking for a Greg. I had Greg make the phone call for me because I didn't know anyone who I could get some more from. I usually get some from him, but he said his homie had some, so how much?" she asked.

My mind was blown the fuck away that this sophisticated woman wanted to buy an ounce of weed. She looked more like a good ass church girl, and it was hard to believe this chick knew

10

anything about drugs.

I told her the price for the weed. She reached into her purse and didn't hesitate in handing me the money. In return, I reached over to give her an ounce of weed. Our fingertips touched during the exchange. Shawty had some smooth skin. I could just imagine how she could work a dick up and down. Our eyes met once again and for about two and half seconds we stared at each other. Once again, I was tripping off her magnificent beauty. As she tucked it away in her purse, my eyes fell on her chest and I saw those light-skinned round tits gleaming in the sun. Trailing my eyes down her curves, I also noticed how thick she was. Ms. Fletcher had to be at least thirty-three. I was twenty-five, but I was thinking that I could easily handle all of that voluptuous grown woman.

"Thanks, bae, it's been nice doing business with chu."

"My name isn't bae. It's Harmony," she snapped with a bit of attitude before turning away and shoving her key in the door.

"Hey, let me holla at chu for a minute," I called out to her from the window of my car. But she didn't even look back. She just slid into her 2015 Honda Civic Coupe and closed the got damn door.

"Yeah, better take yo' fine ass on foe I be pumping all in them guts," I said as I bobbed my head in time to the music, before looking behind me and merging into the late afternoon traffic. Bitches like that make me sick, Bozzee ass.

CHAPTER 2
HARMONY

I pulled up to the Alexander on Ponce apartment situated in Midtown Atlanta after I stopped by my favorite Chinese restaurant, Mu Lan Chinese, in Four Square on my way home. Today had been a gruesome day at Parkside Elementary School where I taught fifth grade students.

There were some bad ass kids in my class with absolutely no home training, none whatsoever. The parents weren't any better when they came marching in the classroom to defend their bad ass kids. Spare the rod, spoil the child, was a true quote to live by. Some of these parents could really take heed of the saying.

I sat there a minute and thought about the guy with the come fuck me eyes and kissable lips that sold me the weed that I needed to calm my nerves.

"Damn. I wish he was just a little bit older," I said as reached for my bag of fried rice and fried dumplings before getting out of my car. The car doors automatically locked behind me as I proceeded toward the stairs that led to my apartment. My heels clacked against the cement in a rhyming fashion as I switched towards my apartment building. I stopped mid-step on the stairs when I saw who was sitting at the top of the staircase. "Byron, why in the world are you here?" I asked him before resuming my walk up the stairs.

"I'm here to see you, baby. I thought that since tonight is Friday we could go out to eat or go catch a movie. We could do anything you want to do," he added as his eyes inspected me from head to toe. He rubbed his hands together and licked his lips sexily.

A couple of months ago, that would have turned me on and

had my thighs wrapped around his waist in a heartbeat as he fucked the shit out of me, but not any longer. Now when I looked at him, all that I felt was disgust.

I stopped just below the stair where Byron was sitting. He suddenly stood up to his full height to peer down at me. "Byron, I haven't seen you in at least three months and we've been broken up even longer. What gives you the right to just show up at my apartment unannounced like this?" I asked with a slight irritation in my voice.

"Sweetheart, you're still not ready to forgive me for one tiny mistake? I fucked up one damn time and you put me in the dog house for months. What more do I have to do before you forgive me?" His tone raised a notch as he threw up his hands and pleaded.

"We can't go back Byron. It's just too late. Once my trust in a person is gone, it's gone," I said as I pushed past Byron and walked the rest of the way up the stairs. I put my key in the lock to unlock my door. I really wasn't interested in what Byron's lame ass had to say anyway. He fucked up one time that I know of. I wouldn't take the chance to think he wouldn't fuck up again.

"Come on, Harmony! Shit, everybody makes mistakes sometimes. I swear to you that it will never happen again." He ran up the steps and I looked over my shoulder.

"The mistake, Byron, was when you brought your ass over here to my apartment to screw another woman in my bed. How fucked up is that?" I turned and shouted at him. "You better be glad that I didn't tell my brother the real reason that I broke up with your lame ass, or you wouldn't be standing here pestering me today," I added.

My older brother, Markus, was the Chief of Police of the Atlanta Fulton County Police Department. I knew bringing Markus up would definitely shake him up. There weren't too many people that were brave enough to cross my brother.

"You think Markus scares me, Harmony?" Byron tried to put up a brave front, but I could tell by the tick in his right eye that the mention of my brother's name scared him to death.

My brother was no ordinary cop. He's the kind of man that would stare a gun right in the eye and if he wasn't killed, he would take that same gun and beat the perp half to death with his own gun. My brother was wild, and no police uniform would domesticate him, but I was glad that he was my big brother. He always looked out for me more than anyone ever had.

"Why do you have to go bringing up your brother in this shit, Harmony? All I wanted to do was to take you out to dinner." He placed his hand over his forehead and paced around the balcony. I could have brought up the fact that Byron had never let me come over to his apartment, but I really didn't even care anymore.

"As you can see, I already have my dinner and the only movies that I will be watching tonight are on Netflix. I'm sorry if you feel like you've wasted your time by coming over here, so don't do it again," I warned him, before walking through my apartment door. "And, Byron," I said as I turned once again to face him.

"Yes," he answered with a hopeful expression on his handsome chocolate face.

"A word of advice to keep in mind, the next woman that you get, don't be bringing thots to her home and fucking them in her bed and don't fucking lie to her. And to think I loved your sneaky, conniving ass," I said before I slammed the door in his no good, cheating ass face. If he kept bothering me, I would be sure to sic Markus on his ass to teach him a lesson in respect and manners. I had to throw away a perfectly good mattress and buy me another one all because of his callous actions. That in itself made him deserve a good ass beat down.

I breathed in and exhaled to shake off of my unplanned and unwanted encounter with my ex. Byron being here when I arrived left a bitter taste in my mouth. I kicked off my heels and let my toes sink down in the soft beige carpet on my living room floor, before moving on to the kitchen to set my food down on the kitchen table. Wasting my precious thoughts on Byron would be a waste of my motherfucking time.

I really needed to take a shower and relax so that I would be able to enjoy my food. I retraced my steps and walked up the spiral open room staircase towards my bedroom. Once inside the bedroom, I started to shed my clothes and left them in a trail as I made my way to the bathroom.

Barefoot and naked, I walked over to the shower to adjust the temperature of the water. Once the water was how I wanted it, I stepped under the dual shower head to let the water beat away the troubles of my day, and that included Byron Martin.

After finishing my shower, I stepped from the shower to wrap up in a big, fluffy towel to dry off. I moisturized my skin before walking over to my dresser drawer to remove a pair of red boy shorts and a cotton tee-shirt to get comfortable in. I walked back down the stairs feeling much more refreshed than I had earlier.

Feeling free and single, I walked over to the end table where I had laid my purse previously to remove the plastic bag full of weed. I had picked up the habit of smoking weed during my early years in college. If Markus knew how much I loved to smoke weed, he would surely have a fit. But what he didn't know couldn't hurt him.

I sat down on my leather sofa and proceeded to roll my blunt with perfect precision. I licked the length of the blunt once I got it rolled just the way I wanted it, sat back, and fired it up. I let out a sigh after my first puff.

"Damn, there's nothing like some good ass weed," I said and walked over to the stereo to turn on my favorite station before walking to the kitchen to heat up my food. Whoever the young, fine guy was that sold me this shit, I needed to personally thank him.

If he wasn't so young, my thirty-three-year-old ass would have given him my cell phone number. *Damn his tattoo was sexy.* I thought about the way it looked on his face. His hazel eyes and thick kissable lips had my other set of lips weeping, but I couldn't let him know that at the time. I knew better. All of these young guys were players, out looking for a good time, and I didn't need the drama or the games. With Byron now in my past, I had gotten past all of that and I really wanted me a man to love me for me who would stay faithful to me.

I had no time for that baby mama drama or an unsurmountable array of thots running behind a delectable looking guy like him. Maybe I should have gotten his name though, so I could have called him personally for me some more of this fiyah ass shit. *Damn.* I coughed as I took another healthy puff and removed my food from the microwave.

Through a fuzzy gaze, I sat there in my panties and tee and smoked me a blunt until it was down to the roach. I was far from an old maid, but damn, here I was home alone on another Friday night. I needed to get a life outside of work and have some fun for a change. It had been a while since I'd been out and had some real fun. It would be Saturday tomorrow. Maybe I should visit the mall and call up my friend Trisha to see if she wanted to tag alone.

She was always trying to get me to go out clubbing with her to one place or another. She would be glad that I was finally agreeing to take her up on her offer. I thought about my plans as I stuffed the last fried dumpling in my mouth. I cleaned off my kitchen table and put away the leftover food in the refrigerator before going to retrieve my cell phone. I decided to call Trisha tonight and put my plans in motion before I changed my mind.

CHAPTER 3
THUG

That night, I went back to the crib and counted up. Including the bags and that ounce to ole girl, in my first day back on the grind, I had made a lil over five hunnad. Shit was cool. I sat on the end of the chair and rolled up a blunt. The only thing a nigga really needed was some pussy to lay up in.

"And I'm shining bright cause I'm really grinding." I sat back and started rapping that Gates shit until I found it on the mixtape app on my phone. By the time the song started playing for real, I was already feeling some type of stunt shit. It had been a long ass time since I'd went out and enjoyed myself.

"They asked me if I was high. I said really real," as the song played on, I sung that shit. I knew right then I was gonna hit up the mall, drop about a bando on some Giuseppe's, and another couple hunnad on some jeans, then stop by the Arabs store and cop a fresh black tee. I switched positions and wondered how I was gone finesse this little situation to get ole girl number though. Since Greg was getting weed from him and ole girl came through that connect, Gator was gone flex on me if I mentioned it to him.

"Where the hell you been all day? I told yo' ass to take out that trash. Smell like duke and feet in this motherfucker." My sister was always talking shit. I hated crashing at her crib.

"Co Co, ain even been in this motherfucker but two days. Got damn. Probably yo stanking ass tracks. You the one walking round this motherfucker gluing in hair pieces and shit."

"Probably them funky ass blunt and shit you be rolling. Nigga, two days... Shid that's long enough to get some funk stirred up in this motherfucker. You been sitting yo' ass on my couch,

17

eating, and taking a shit. All my tissue gone. You been watching *Love & Hip Hop* and all the free shit you wanna. Now you sit over there and count up ya lil money like you got damn Nino Brown and shit. All I ask you to do was—" By the time her ass got to that, I had already tuned her fish mouth ass out. Sometimes my sister Co Co be on that bullshit. Thinking she all that just cause she owned her own salon and shit. I was gone take out the damn trash. I had just forgot the shit this morning when I went over to Gator's.

"Man, ain even been here. I been over to Gator's in the day time, but ahite, man, cool. Just make sure you don't climb yo got damn teeth on my French fries no moe when I get some." Sometimes we went at it like cats and dogs, but on the real, I loved my sister even though she thought she was the shit. I rarely came over her crib, mainly cause I knew we would get into it. Plus, I be too busy trapping.

"Boy, gone wit dat." She waved her hand and jumped on the phone, probably with her best friend, Sweetie. "Guh, for real. Where he stay?" I heard her voice fading as I picked up the bag and closed the door. I went out back and placed the bag of trash in the can. For a minute, I just stood there thinking about some real shit. I needed to get my own spot. It was only one way to make that shit come faster though. I needed more clientele and I needed to get off this pack, keep re-upping, and stacking my bread. Thinking about all that was going on made me smoke another blunt. I was not about to spend my weekend listening to her duke mouth ass. It was even more reason I needed to go out and enjoy myself some. Fuck it. I decided to go to the club tomorrow night.

***

"Aye let a' nigga get towel or some,"

"Thug, you know where they at, don't do that," Co Co replied. I knew where they were.

I was just fucking with her. After getting a towel and face rag, I closed the bathroom door and shed my clothes. I turned on the water and stepped into the shower as a restless sigh left my lips. It had been one hell of a day.

"Fuck, man." I'd been getting my grizzy on and fucking with them crummy ass niggas who always wanted to say yo' bag was too little and shit. *Bum ass niggas.*

Only motherfucker who didn't talk shit was Ms. Harmony Fletcher. I would really like to fuck with her the long way. Shit, if I was serving her on the regular, a nigga would get a chance to run up in that. For a minute, I thought about her sexy ass voice. It was soft and seductive. I wondered how it would sound if she said my name while we were fucking and how it sounded in a soft moan. I remembered how we touched hands during the exchange. She had some very soft and yellow skin. Suddenly, I remembered just how damn good those hands felt as I washed myself. I grabbed more of the liquid soap and squeezed some in the palm of my hand.

"Is that what I think it is?" I remembered her soft and sexy voice. I bit my lip.

"Yeah, motherfucker, it's a ten-inch dick. Want some?" I wanted to say, while I focused on the way she leaned into the car.

"How much?"

"Man, fuck the weed let a nigga get some of that pretty ass mouth."

"What if someone catches us?"

"I really don't care if we get caught. Get yo ass in."

"Okay, daddy." I imagined her climbing into my car with a tone sounding kittenish and sexy. She got in the car and closed the door. "What do you want me to do first, big daddy?"

I whipped it out. "Shid, go get it," I said leaning back and stretching my arm over the seat and waiting for her hands to run down my pants naughtily.

As I imagined it all happening, I made faster strokes up and down my shaft in the shower with the liquid soap. Jacking off and thinking about Ms. Fletcher was making me about to cum. I wondered what she felt like for real. It had been a long time since a nigga had smashed something and I could use a good nut right then in that shower.

"Damn you big," she whispered, taking off her bra and rubbing her tits. She cupped one and sucked the nipple slowly. When she saw I wanted it, she licked her lips and stared at it. Ms. Harmony was wild and dangerously looking at what she wanted and I sure as hell wanted to give it to her.

"You gone come for me, daddy?" she said seductively while sucking her thump and batting her eyes devilishly.

I felt that first quake run through me as I ran my thumb across my pee-hole and teased it and imagined her tongue lapping the center of it. I squirted more soap for extra lubrication and my hand shoved itself along the shaft of my dick brutally. I would lay off the teasing because I'd almost just nutted. I wanted to save it a little while longer so I fucked the O-shape of my hand, thinking about how sexy those lips were and I imagined her talking to me in that naughty little tone. I could feel the tightness of my hand squeezing like Harmony's mouth would be if she actually sucked me off. For the next few seconds, I stroked only the head and thought about those lips wrapped around it tightly. It was slippery and wet as I pounded the palm of my hand thinking about her.

"Hell yea I'm about to cum. I feel it. Your mouth feels so damn good to me, baby. I'm not pulling it out either I'mma buss right in yo' mouth." When I said that, she smirked mischievously and went down on me again repeatedly almost as if she wanted me to cum for her.

"Mmmm, you taste so good. Don't take it out. I want you to cum in my mouth. I wanna taste it." She slurped and smacked her lips and continued to suck on just the head.

"Look atchu, turn the fuck up then witcho grown ass," I said and she giggled a little.

"Turn down for what? Just hurry up and come in my mouth, baby. I

gotta get back to my class," she begged. Just imagining her grown ass beg for me to cum inside her mouth had me ready to squirt. That anticipation made my pre-cum skeet and a long urge to cum ran all over me. I jacked off for about ten more minutes imaging her lips snug around my dick.

"Ole freaky ass hoe," I yelled and tried to suppress that nut, but Harmony had some plump ass lips.

Nut shot out all over my wrist and fingers. I looked down at the shower floor and my sperm was running down the drain. "Got damn, Harmony. I want you bad."

CHAPTER 4
HARMONY

Trisha and I left the Lennox Square mall loaded down with more bags than we intended to carry. "Gurl, I'm so glad you called me last night to suggest we go shopping. Dayquan was about to get on my last nerve with his shit," she said, speaking of her lazy no working ass boyfriend.

Trisha Carter and I went to college together. She had a little bit of ghetto and wildness in her, which drew me to her right away. She was the type of girl who didn't mince her words. When she smelled bullshit, she would call you out on it. She didn't care who you were, even if you were the President of the United States. That's why I never understood why Trisha took so much shit off her live in sorry ass boyfriend, Dayquan Riley. She went out to work five days a week, sometimes six if her job as a Biological Technician with Grady Memorial Hospital called for it. Trisha was brilliant, but also ghetto-fabulous when she wanted to be, and I loved her like a sister.

"I'm glad that I finally decided to call you, too. It was about time I got out of that apartment and stop acting like an old lady," I told her and my tone tapered down a notch. I decided not to voice my true thoughts about her boyfriend at the moment. There was no way I was going to chance ruining our day by bringing up that she could do a lot better than the likes of Dayquan Riley.

I hit the wireless remote to unlock my Honda Civic Coupe, so we could place our bags in the trunk. "I know just the place for us to turn up tonight." Trisha slid a sly glance my way.

"Trisha, what are you up to? I just want to go somewhere nice and laid back…Maybe order me a drink or two and maybe even do some dancing," I added and closed the trunk.

"There will be plenty of dancing and drinking where I'm thinking of taking us tonight. It may even remind us of some of the places we used to get into when we snuck out of our dorm room in college. You remember the fun we used to have, right?" She popped her gum loudly as she waited for my reply. I opened the driver's side door and slid in. Once Trisha was in, I glanced at her.

"Yasss, I remember those days well, but I've matured since then, and so have you." I gave her a serious look. "I don't need to be going anywhere where fights can pop off at any moment and gun shots either, for that matter. I don't need to be running for my life. Besides, you know good and well if the police show up and I get arrested for some foolishness, guess who's the first mouth I will hear about it?" I asked her.

"Markus with his fine ass self," she supplied. "I don't know why he be all up in your business the way he does. He needs to let me loosen him up a bit, maybe he would seem more human instead of acting like the terminator all of the time. He has that good cop, bad cop persona down to a tee."

As we buckled up, I laughed at Trisha's description of Markus. She was mostly right about him, so I had to agree. "You're right, Trisha. Markus be on some kind of power trip at times. I love him to life though. I just wish he would stop treating me like I was twelve instead of the thirty something year old grown woman that I am. There are only two years separating us and he acts like he's my damn daddy!"

"I feel you on that girlfriend. But don't worry about where I'm taking you. Everything will be kosher. I promise you. There will be a party going on at Club Blue Sapphire. You know all the high ballers will be hanging out there. My friend Neiman got us seats in the V.I.P. section. I've already texted him to confirm. What do you think about that? You know I got this. Your girl knows how to party," she said, putting emphasis on the word "party."

"Do you know how hard it is to get in Club Blue Sapphire?" I asked. The multi-level nightclub was one of the hottest spots around. I started the ignition as I waited for Trisha's reply.

"Of course, I know it. Why do you think I called Neiman after we got through talking last night? You know that Neiman has been a hairstylist and make-up artist for the rich and famous for quite some time now. He comes in contact with all sorts of people that do favors on the regular for him. The only thing is, he wants to tag along."

I gave her a sideways look, as I stopped at a traffic light. Because Trisha and I both knew that Neiman could be a little out there in the flamboyant way he dressed. He wore more make-up than Trisha and I did most times. I didn't have anything against Trisha's friend, but I just wanted tonight to be low key. I didn't need to bring unwanted attention to myself and Neiman had a way of bringing attention everywhere he went. I had always been a low key kind of girl, and that didn't change the older I got.

"Girl, don't you worry none about Neiman. He promised me that he would be on his best behavior. I told him how you are and he completely understands," she assured me as a car pulled up next to us and stopped at the light as well.

"What do you mean you talked to Neiman about me?" I slid her a narrowed eyed look before I returned my attention to the roadway, since the traffic signal had turned green.

"Calm down, Harmony. You need to loosen up a bit instead of being so serious and uptight all of the time. I didn't say anything bad about you because there is nothing bad to say about you, my good friend. I just bluntly told Neiman that he couldn't be acting a fool because you didn't get down like that. I'm driving tonight by the way because I'm going to make sure that you get a drink or two in your system before we go out tonight," she said as the city dashed by in the window behind her.

"I'm not getting blasted," I warned her.

"Who said anything about getting blasted, Harmony? You just need enough alcohol in your system to let go and have a good time."

"You're right," I finally agreed and dropped the subject about the forthcoming night and talked about something else until I dropped her off at her apartment.

"I'll pick you up around nine o'clock tonight so be ready," Trisha said as she got out of the car.

I assured her that I would be ready and popped the trunk for her to retrieve her shopping bags. I gave her a final wave before backing out of the parking space and merged into the busy traffic. Tonight I would finally have a chance to meet some new people and I couldn't wait.

CHAPTER 5
HARMONY

Trisha arrived promptly at nine o'clock like she said she would. I was also ready like I promised to be. "Guuurl! You are looking too good in that jumpsuit! Aren't you glad I talked you into getting it?" Trisha perked up a pretty girl pose with her lips when I got into her brand new Acura RLX.

I looked down at my body-hugging, black jumpsuit and had to admit that it fit me like a glove and showed off all my sensual curves. "Thank you. You look great as well." I admired her new outfit and complimented her on her great taste in clothes. "Did Dayquan get upset when you told him you were going out with me tonight?"

"Gurl, no. I would have given him the business if he had. He was getting dressed to leave out himself. If I had stayed home, I would have been there by my damn self anyway," she admitted and with a sudden excitement in her tone she sat up as if she'd just remembered something. "Oh, I forgot to tell you," she said taking one hand off of the steering wheel to snap her fingers. "I gave Dayquan an ultimatum."

"What kind of ultimatum?" I sat my ass up too and stared at her profile as she drove down the highway. Trisha knew how to spill some tea.

"I told his ass that he had one month to find a job or I would be kicking him out of my apartment." She smacked her lips and rolled her neck. "And I told his ass I don't have any children and it's about time he stopped acting like a child and be about his grown man business," she replied with a head motion.

"Say what? Girl, you told his ass right. Trisha, I can't believe you did it. Shit I don't blame you. You are too intelligent of a woman to have to put up with Dayquan's crap anyways. I'm so proud of you, because you deserve better. Dayquan really needs to get his act together," I said.

Most women may have thought I was jealous because my friend had a man and I didn't, but Trisha and I was better than that so she knew my comment was coming from a good place in my heart.

"You're damn straight I deserve better. I always knew I did, but the heart loves who the heart loves and I truly love Dayquan Riley. But you know what Harmony?" she asked, throwing me a quick and serious glance.

"What?" I gave her an expectant look.

"I sho love myself more," she stated with defiance.

"For sho," I exclaimed. "I wish I had a drink right now because I would toast to what you just said."

Trisha cupped her hand over her mouth, but couldn't hide the burst out laughter. "Now you know you ain't said nothing but a word. Girl, look in the glove compartment and pull out those two miniature bottles of Pink Moscato that I stopped by the liquor store and got on my way to pick you up."

I joined her in laughter as she turned up the music to Rhianna's song "Work" and I opened up both bottles of Pink Moscato. I handed her one and I had one for myself. I touched my bottle to hers since she needed to keep her eyes on the night's traffic.

"Here's to a great time tonight and to you finding a better man or Dayquan becoming a better man." I had to throw that in there for effect.

"I'll toast to that, but wait, I have one more toast to make," she said.

"Go ahead," I waited with my bottle still touching

27

hers.

"To you, Harmony Fletcher, may you find your dream man tonight. Someone that will rock your world and then some, because I know you gotta be horny as hell since you and Byron's cheating ass broke up."

"Okay," I laughed. "I will drink to and admit that I'm horny as hell, but let me just be clear about this. Harmony Fletcher don't need no man. I have a D set of batteries and BOB at home waiting for me and he don't come with a set of problems like a lot of men do!"

"Gurl, you know you crazy as hell, right?" She didn't even wait until I answered her question, she just kept on talking. "Because let me tell you that I've tried BOB too, but there is nothing like a real dick feeling up a woman's pussy, stirring those juices around, sooner or later, you gone need some penetration," she stated and pulled into a parking space at Club Blue Sapphire.

I couldn't even argue what she said because deep down I knew she was right. So I just sat there and turned up my miniature bottle of Pink Moscato before getting of the car.

"Hey, you two. Over here!" Neiman hollered and waved his arms over his head to get our attention.

"Thank you, God," I whispered to Trisha. Neiman looked normal tonight and I just had to thank God for small favors.

"Hey, Neiman," Trisha and I both greeted him with a kiss to each of his cheeks. That's the way he always greeted friends. I smiled at his easy going nature because he really was a nice guy.

"Look who has just arrived!" Neiman said as I looked at the long ass line of patrons waiting to get into Club Blue Sapphire. "Miss Trisha and Miss Harmony you better know it. Now we can get this party started for real honey. Turn up! Follow me guys." He led us to the front of the line.

He may have lost his flamboyant clothes for tonight, I thought, *but he sure hadn't lost the switch in his walk.* I placed one of my hands up to my forehead and followed, "Lord, help me Jesus."

CHAPTER 6
THUG

Through my speakers, I could hear that Space Age Pimpin by 8 ball MJG beating soulfully, *I'll be yo obliged if you step outside because my ride is awaiting our date and, of steak and a night cap we mating.* Sometimes I loved listening to that throwback shit. As I came to the light, I remembered I needed to stop and get a rillo, so I pulled in to the nearest gas station. The music was still paying when I opened the door and got out.

The way you made a nigga laugh
I had to getcha
And when I saw that ass pass
I had to hitcha

With my strap under my shirt, I closed the door and left my car running and went into the store. It was a few chicks in line getting some mints and bottled water.

"Oh nie, ya'll don't need no green do it?" I reached in my pants and pulled out a Ziploc containing small bags of weed in it. "Dis dat fye." I held it out. The smallest girl turned to face me, while the others acted scared as fuck.

"Let me get a bag," she held out a ten and I handed her the green. "Girl, you don't even know his ass," one of the girls blurted.

"Aye, lil momma, they call me Thug. Put my number in yo phone when you need some more hit me up," I gave the short chick my number and stuck a bird at the other motherfucker. They walked out of the store and I shoved the green back into my pocket. "Aye let me get two cigarillos."

The Arab was trying to make small talk and shit though. "You like pickle?"

30

"Hell naw ion want no motherfucking pickle. Just give me the got damn rillo bruh, damn." He slid it on the counter and I gave him the ten the chick just gave me and he gave me change. Just as I was handing him the money, I got a phone call. It was from Gator. "Look, ain coming to the spot tonight. I'm on my way to the club bruh, but what's hannan?" I said, but a loud and hysterical feminine voice came blaring through the phone.

"Twelve came through. They got Gator, but they didn't find the green. It's like ten pounds of that stuff lying here and it stinks real bad Thug. I don't know what to do with it."

"Lock the motherfucking door and don't open that bitch for no one you hear me Bree? No one! I'm on the way." On everything I love, I left the rillos on the counter and ran the fuck out the store. I couldn't go to no fucking club. I needed to get to this weed.

***

After weaving through traffic for twenty minutes, I was finally there.

"Bree, open the door, it's Thug!" I yelled banging on the front door with my fist. My other hand was holding the banger directly at the front door. I heard the latch come undone. She opened the door and looked over my shoulder. "Why you all spooked and shit?" I asked brushing past her and walking in. I lowered the gun and I locked it behind me. "Where the green?"

"Cause, nigga, twelve was deep as hell. It's back there in my room. Oh my God, that shit stinks so bad Thug." She pointed towards her bedroom. I had known which way was Bree's bedroom from coming over from time to time, but I'd never been in there. I tucked my banger back under my shirt. When I walked in, the smell hit me too.

"Got damn, this shit funky than a motherfucker." I held up a pound and sniffed. "This that loud pack bruh." My eyes shimmered with a gritty ass gleam. All I could think about right then was how much motherfucking cake I could make off it. "What happened?"

"Gator had just re-upped. He got a call and went to meet somebody down the street and next thing I knew, twelve pulled up. They hopped out and started putting him in handcuffs then shoved him in the car," Bree said and I finally lowered the pound of loud that was in my hand.

"So they ain't come in here?"

"No. They pulled up on him down the street. It was hella po-pos out there though." Bree was like my little sister and Gator would want me to look out for her. They momma died when Bree was twelve. Gator was all she really had. I pulled up the JailBase app on my phone and looked up Byron Martin. I glanced at the phone a few times just to be sure, but nothing was pulling up yet.

"Check, Imma stay here witchu for a while until we figure out this little situation with Gator. Don't even wor bout' it. Imma take care you, my nigga. I got this shit." When I said that, Bree fell into me and her head collapsed on my chest.

"Thank you Thug," she said in a very low and innocent tone. I knew right then what I had to do. I needed to go touch base with a few niggas that move weight so I could get off this weed. I needed to go down to Club Blue Sapphire like right now.

"I'll be back." I promised and cocked my brim over my eye. "And don't open the door for nobody. You got that?" I emphasized.

"I got it," she said and slammed the door behind me. I could hear the deadbolt clicking into place as Bree secured the house.

32

CHAPTER 7
THUG

The whole ride there, a nigga didn't listen to shit but the wind as it sifted through the window. I had some fucking business to handle. I glanced over at the pistol on my seat and the choppa on the floor. *A motherfucker flex, a motherfucker snore.*

When I pulled up to the club, the line was filled with niggas and bitches from all over the city. My mind wasn't on no pussy, none of that dumb shit, so I didn't even pay them hoes no attention. I just needed to holler at a few of these niggas and let them know I had some fye ass weed. Everybody knew me and Gator was thick so that wasn't a prob to get it popping. Motherfuckers wouldn't fuck with me just on the strength of that alone. A lot of his clientele was mainly niggas that copped a pound here or there, others got a half of pound and some a few ounces. It all depended on who they were and how much clientele they had of their own.

I grabbed my pistol and got out. By the time I reached the back of the line, I realized if a nigga wanted to get in soon he was gone have to Debo some shit.

"Fuck on bruh," I pulled up my pants slightly and brushed passed a few niggas and bitches. When a nigga did flex, I lifted my brim and gave his ass one look that told him everything about Thug that he needed to know. With my brim tilted to the left, I made my way up the line, but like always, it was one motherfucker to look at you crazy as fuck.

"Thug, you still causing problems in the city? I thought yo ass was locked up, nigga." When I finally noticed who it was, we dapped hands.

"What it do, Rod D, my neezy?"

33

"Shit, my guh just broke up wit me so a nigga juh out here tryna catch some new pussy." Rod D had a bad ass bitch name Sweetie Frost. She was friends with my Co Co, but the bitch wouldn't let nobody get up in that pussy but this nigga, Rod D.

"Fasho, aye. I know you fucking wit Zoe and nem now, but I got some that good shit if you need to re-up,"

"Aye, you know when I come through I need the whole thang, I don't…"

"I got my weight up nigga, I got you." When I said that, a gleam shot into his eyes.

"Bet dat, Imma swing through. You still be posted at Gator crib?"

"Yeah," I replied and with a head nod I kept it moving. I sold a few more bags in line and by the time I had made my way to the door I noticed the way that cornball ass security was looking at me. "Yo', you gotta motherfucking problem?" I removed the hat from my head, but the nigga only stared then looked away at some chick who was trying to get his attention. From behind, shawty had a lot of ass. I wasn't even thinking bout no bitch forrealla, but shawty made me do a double take. She was wearing a black jumpsuit that cupped her juicy ass perfectly.

For a second, she motioned with her hands and seemed to be getting this cornball ass nigga to lighten up a little. She had long, wavy hair and whatever she was saying made this nigga laugh, but by the time I walked up to enter, his gaze suddenly changed.

"Aye, my man, you can't get in. I see you jumping the line and shit. Plus, your attire doesn't comply with our dress code." He held out his hand. I looked down at my black tee and gold chain.

"Bruh, you ain seen me do shit." A large vein shot up the side of my neck as I stood facing him off. He looked the other way and spoke more-so towards the air.

"Like I said, you ain't getting in." Before I knew it, my tone and hand both rose a notch, but before I could even snap on his ass, the chick turned around and grabbed me by my gold chain and pressed her finger to my lips.

CHAPTER 8
HARMONY

"Aye my man, you can't get in," the bouncer had said as he mean mugged whoever he was talking to behind me.

I saw you jumping the line and shit. Plus, your attire doesn't comply with our dress code," he continued.

Chills automatically went down my spine when the person replied. *I know that voice.* Being curious, my head swirled around. That was when I knew for sure that it was indeed the same guy I got that fiyah ass weed from the other day.

I looked him up and down as he stood there tall and muscular, his hat tilted to the side shielding those translucent eyes. He was hella cute in his black tee and gold chain. By the look in his eyes, I knew some shit was going to go down from his defensive stance and the tone of his voice. I had seen the same intense look in Markus' eyes on numerous occasions. He probably had weed on him too and a pistol with no license, and if the police got involved, it would be just another sad case of a brother getting in trouble.

"Bruh, you ain't seen me do shit," he continued to argue. So I did the only thing that I could do to damper what could have ended in a volatile confrontation.

"Hey boo! What in the world took you so long? I've been waiting on you? Neiman said to tell you if I see you to hurry, we're about to toast to a great success on our new adventure together." I pulled him by his gold chain.

I knew that I'd heard that sexy ass voice somewhere. I didn't know why the hell I got the sudden idea to defuse a situation that had absolutely nothing to do with me in the first place though.

Tatted up and all, his face suddenly relaxed as he looked

36

down at me. Thug leaned into my grasp willingly. For a moment, his eyes lingered on the swell of my breasts before they traveled down further. That look he gave me sent an electrical shock all over me. A light dawned in his eyes and a sly smile finally parted the sides of his face, revealing the deepest dimples I'd ever seen. I noticed the gleam that suddenly appeared on his lips when his eyes finally collided with mine again.

"Bae, I told yo ass I was on my way. You didn't have to sweat it. Shid, Thug word is good always, believe dat," he said, playing along. He then had the audacity to give me a cocky ass hug and another kiss but this one landed on my cheek.

Damn, that Moscato that I drank in the car must be rearing its head because when he hugged me and gave me a kiss, my panties became wet. I squeezed my legs together to quell the sudden pulsing of my clit against my thong.

"Harmony, who is that?" Trisha walked up from behind me and whispered in my ear.

"I'll explain later," I turned to her and spoke in a low voice.

"Oh, this nigga with you and Neiman?" the bouncer asked me.

"Aye my nigga, the name is Thug. Use it," he stated with a slouch and then pulled up the crotch of his jeans. That gritty persona he had just did something to me.

"Yes, he's with us," Neiman had come to stand beside me and Trisha as he eyed Thug up and down.

I quickly looked at Thug to see another frown appear on his face as he glanced Neiman's way. Trisha and I knew that Neiman was harmless, but by the look on Thug's face there was a look of controversial in his eyes.

"Come on," I quickly grabbed ahold of Thug's hand. Thug generously paid the admittance fee for us to enter the club and tipped the bouncer an extra hundred.

"If I'd known yo fine ass was gon' be up in this bitch, I

woulda zipped through here sooner," Thug said and secured his grip in the clasp of my hand, but once we were inside, my demeanor changed.

"Ahh, don't take this the wrong way," I turned to him and said as I attempted to pull away from his grasp. "But you do know that we aren't really together? I was just being nice and doing you a favor to get you in here since you did me one the other day. So you can go your way and I'll go mine," I replied hoping that he would get the hint. I pulled away and turned to find a more cheerful and familiar voice.

"Hey!" Trisha came dancing up behind me with Neiman. "Turn up, turn up. Gurl, it's on and poppin' up in here," she said looking around and shrugging her shoulders to the beat. Neiman was sipping from his cup and staring at all the guys as they walked by.

I had to silently agree with Trisha. The music was blasting in the dimly lit club. The mystically placed strobe lights all over the club gave off a bluish hue. The main floor held a wall to wall bar with a dance floor. I looked up to the second level as the bass blared from the surround sound speakers inside the walls. There were people glued together and enjoying themselves. From where I was, I could see couples on the second level of the club dancing and smiling.

"Are we going to stand here all day or are we going to go to the third level to the VIP section?" Neiman asked as he bobbed his head in rhythm to the music.

"I'm with you two," I quickly said in agreement as I tried to totally disengage myself from Thug, who had retrieved my hand and held on to me possessively as if we were truly a couple.

"Shawty, lemme holla atcha for a minute," Thug leaned in and whispered. I felt the brim of his hat brush against my hair as he bent down to whisper in my ear. There was this invisible force surrounding him at all times that just tranquilized me and I didn't know why.

Chills once again ran down my spine and heat settled deep in my pussy's core. *Damn, why was this younger guy affecting me in this way? Snap out of it Harmony Fletcher,* I reprimanded myself with a quickness.

"You coming with us or not, Harmony?" Trisha eyeballed Thug as he held me close to his side.

"Nah, yawl gon' on ahead. Harmony will catch up with ya later." He waved them away like they were a bit of a nuisance, as if I didn't have a say in the matter at all.

I frowned and breathed in deeply. My nostrils were assailed by the spicy scent from his cologne as I stood there. Trisha and Neiman stood in the same spot and waited for my reply.

"I'll catch up with you two in a few minutes. Will that be a problem?" I asked directing my question at Neiman since he was the one that was getting us in the VIP section.

"It's cool. Just take that elevator over there," he pointed to the bank of elevators across the room. "Third floor. I will leave your name at the door," he replied.

"Thanks Neiman. I won't be long."

"Don't worry I ain't gone bite her. Shawty in good hands with Thug, believe dat," he said and before I had even known it, I swatted him on the shoulder.

"Don't be so rude." I warned Thug and paid them a confident smile.

Trisha and Neiman seemed satisfied before they walked away and left me alone with this young Thug.

***

"C'mon let me buy you a drink," he said without waiting for me to agree, as he led me over to the bar. "Watchu want to drink?" he asked and gave me that dangerously passionate stare again.

Those eyes of his would get me in trouble if I wasn't careful.

"I'll have a margarita," I replied before tearing my gaze away from him. I was really still checking him out as he placed our orders with the bartender, but he didn't know it.

Thug pulled of a thick roll of money and paid for them. Once my drink was in hand, Thug indicated he wanted for us to go sit at one of the empty tables. We found one in the corner of the dimly lit club and sat down. I took the straw and stirred it around, hoping to ward off that longing glare he willfully gave.

"Harmony, check this out...It must be fate that we met up at this particular time and place. I'm not gon' beat around the bush or any thang like that, so I'm just gone say this shit. I want you," he admitted as I looked up and stared into his eyes.

"Want me like what?" I asked when I noticed I'd just gotten a text from my girl Trisha asking me if I was okay. I sent her back a text letting her know I was fine and lifted my head to find a set of wet lips in my direct line of vision.

"I wanna fuck." Those words sank into me like an anchor in deep water. I wasn't expecting Thug to be so blunt with his words. My eyes traveled from his lips to his set of eyes that were also staring. That pause in between my reply and his want for my pussy was more than I was prepared for. I finally had to look away from the deep look in his brown eyes. I took a sip of my drink and cleared my throat before I spoke.

"See that's the problem, Thug. I'm not a little girl. I'm a full grown woman. You can't just ask for my pussy like that." I tried to give him a stern look. The same one I bestowed on some of my fifth grade students when I meant what I said, but hell, it wasn't working on him just like it didn't work on some of their hard headed butts. He licked those damn succulent lips of his and my juices ran some more. I would have to go in the restroom and remove my thongs if this heat kept running through me.

"Shid, anyone with eyes can see you're a grown ass woman.

That's just a figure of speech, boo. But get this," he said licking his lips and rubbing his hands together like Birdman.

He looked deep into my eyes again and held his gaze as if he were demanding my attention. I sat up in my seat a little bit straighter, took notice, and listened to what he had to say because even though he was cute, my mind was already made up and there wasn't anything that Thug could do or say to change that.

"I know you heard the old ass sayin' that age ain't nuthin' but a number. I may be younger than you, but that don't mean shit. When yo feelings get involved…" Thug stopped and took a cube of ice from his cup with the tip of his tongue. He formed a breathtaking arch in the center and allowed the piece of ice to glide over the grooves of his tongue until it disappeared. "You have to obey those feelings and I think a nigga like me can make you feel real good, whether it's casual or even sexual," he said with confidence in his voice and looked away uninterestedly. "But you may not be ready for all that so, ah, just tell me a lil bit about yoself, Ms. Harmony," he suddenly changed the subject, picked us his glass, and took a big swallow.

"Ahh, hmm, there is really nothing to tell. I work, I come home, bathe, eat, and go to bed. I live a very boring life, Thug," I sadly admitted.

"You smoke that gan too," he smirked.

"Yeah, I smoke that gan as you call it," I chuckled with him. Quickly our smiles faded and Thug seemed more interested in me again.

"I can't believe a beautiful sexy ass woman like yoself is living a boring life though. Somebody running up that ass. Where yo man at?" he asked without blinking.

"I did have one of those, but I don't any longer."

"What dat nigga do? I already kno he did sum scurvy ass shit by the look in yo eyes," he took another sip from his drink.

41

"Yeah, it was B..." I almost blurted his name and figured it would be less important to even mention, besides, they probably didn't even know each other. "Yeah it was his fault, but I'm not dwelling on his cheating ass," I said, getting angry at how I had allowed myself to love and trust Byron in the way that I did. Byron had always been discreet about things. He had told me he had a job selling cars at the car lot, but I found out that wasn't true. He had never even let me come to his so called apartment, neither did he ever introduce me to any of his friends. All he did was lie to me. I placed my cup on the table. "I don't want to talk about my ex any longer, and to be honest, I don't even want to talk about me anymore. By the way, how old are you, Thug?"

"I'm old enough to kno when a lady ain't being fucked right. Shid, I'm old enough to know what I want and I want you, Harmony. I want that pussy you got in between yo legs." I sat my cup down on the table after his blunt words...I blinked a time or two before I found my voice to and spoke again.

"What did you just say?" I asked shocked once again by his declaration. No one had ever spoken to me this directly before.

"Don't be flexing like you deaf and shit. I'm sure you very acquainted with the vocabulary. Ya heard me, babe. I want dat pussy. Imma get it too and it ain't shit you can do about it. Now finish yo drink. I got some bizzness I got to handle, but when I'm ready for it, I'mma get it," he said, removing his cell from the clip at his waist. He slid it across the table in front of me. "You gone love it when dat hotline bling and say incoming from my nigga, Thug."

I sat there and looked at him and then the cell phone lying on the table in front of me. *How the hell was he going to boss me around in the way he did and demand for me to give him my number?* The more I stared into those dreamy eyes of his, I decided to test the waters. *What could it hurt? Right? One time only and then I'm done.*

"Here," I said after I put my number into his cell phone. I

slid it back across the table to him. Our fingers brushed when he reached for it and I felt it again, that rebellious surge of something so unexplainable.

It radiated from his fingertips to my own. I jerked my fingers back and swallowed nervously. "I don't mean to be rude, but I better get back to my friends," I said standing up from the table.

"Imma take you up," he said taking one last gulp from his tumbler and stood as well. I don't know if it was the music, or that got damn margarita, but something had me going.

Damn he was fine. I looked at the wide expanse of his chest and wondered what he would look like with his tee-shirt off. I would definitely have to make use of BOB when I got home later tonight.

"You don't have to go with me. I can find my friends on my own."

"I know you can, but imma make sure you get there safely. Lotta pussy niggas lurking round here" he replied with a smirk on his face.

I walked ahead of him towards the bank of elevators. I think he purposely walked behind me so he could watch the way my ass jiggled in my black jumpsuit. I looked back and sure enough his eyes were glued to the sway of my backside. He looked up into my eyes and smirked, but said nothing.

The doors closed and we rode up in the elevator in relative silence, but I could feel his eyes on me because mine were on him. Suddenly, Thug reached around me and hit the stop button on the elevator.

"Ahh, what the hell are you doing?" I gave him a wide eyed look.

"I'm doing what I wanted to do since the first time yo ass strolled up to my car with that bossy ass demeanor. You weren't scared to fuck with a real nigga. I like that shit, gurl," he said licking his lips again. "But, ah, I wanna taste yo lips again. They look so good they got a mu'fuckan nigga feeling thirsty." He stepped closer and pushed up on me. I placed both hands upon his chest to shield myself from him.

I gasped for more air as he prowled over me with romantic eyes filled with desire. The gap between us closed as he leaned in letting our chests meet and for a moment. I just stood there simply paralyzed as his lips came closer to mine.

I won't let him kiss me.

That thought dug itself somewhere in the pit of my stomach and settled there. Not only was the presence of him exuding with lustful intimidation, but also the way he smelled had me drifting into another world beyond all rational thinking. In those quick seconds, I wondered how serious he was about kissing me and if he would get violent when I refused. Those feelings, his rude behavior, it all over whelmed me to the point that my breathing had become irregular and out of control.

"Thug I…I can't…"

"Harmony…" His nose brushed against mine and when it did I noticed the tiny scar under his left eye. For a moment I wondered how he got it. My eyes slid back down to those forcible lips that were just about to reach mine. My heartbeat picked up speed and thumped hard as he leaned beyond my resistance. I was sure it was beating hard enough for him to hear it in the quiet elevator with just the two of us enclosed.

"Thug," I finally said again just before his thick lips touched mine, but it was too late. I closed my eyes the moment we kissed and felt something run though me.

"Open up for a real nigga," he instructed and shoved his warm tongue against my lips. I grabbed a hold of his gold chain like it was my lifeline.

I allowed him to get into my mouth, just once to sooth that irresistible urge. Instead of being soothed, I desired even more of him. His taste and smell were a duel assault on my senses. The world around me seemed to stop on its axis. Thug sealed his lips over mine and kissed every cell in my entire body awake. As our mouths came together, he backed me against the elevator wall. Our tongues met again and again colliding and gliding sinfully over each other's, each time seeming like it would be the last, but we couldn't stop. For the next few seconds, our tongues wrestled passionately and intertwined with forbidden intimacy, as he pulled me closer to him. With a hungry urge, he ran his hands over my breast and up my chest until he reached my hair. The rapid throbbing of my clit between my thighs intensified as he pulled and tugged on me roughly.

"Thug?" I backed away and freed the strands of hair from my weary eyes, but he kissed me again.

As I swallowed his kisses, I could hear throwback song of Usher's playing in the background, *I wanna make love in this club, in this club, in this club...I wanna..."*

His leg slid between my thighs to force them apart. The thickness of his erection came in direct contact with my clean shaven wet folds. The clothes that I had on didn't stop me from getting the feel of his massive hard meat that was now grinding against my wet covered mound. Thug mounted my head to the elevator wall as he carried me through a maelstrom of emotions and kissed his way down to the side of my neck.

"Damn, Harmony. We make magic happen. You hear dat song? You hear what the DJ playing?" he asked. By then it was on Jeezy's part of the song.

"I'm whatcha want. I'm whatcha need. Gotcha trap. I set ya free, sexually mentally, physically, emotionally. I'll be like ya medicine, you'll take every dose of me." With my hair matted upon my face, I nodded with my bottom lip tucked.

"This right here...this shit mine," He reached down and felt on my pussy firmly. "I want yo ass spread eagled on a bed right now," he muttered against the side of my neck before he licked my neck from my shoulder blade, to just below my jawbone. I could have easily cummed on the spot as his hands wandered all over my body before coming to settle on my plump ass cheeks.

"Damn, you taste good. I can just imagine how that pussy and ass taste," he squeezed my ass cheeks again and pressed me closer which caused me to grind on his dick some more.

"Thug," I gasped as lustful pleasure begged me to allow him to take me against the wall in the elevator, but common sense finally permeated my brain. "Stop!" I finally found the strength and said. "I can't do this here, and I can't do this with you at all. I don't even know you," I added and stepped away from him to smooth the fly away wavy curls of my hair back down.

"I don't like it, but I understand," he said with drugged unfulfilled eyes.

"Start the elevator please. I'm sure people are waiting to use it."

"I don't give a fuck about dese people, Harmony. You got a nigga ready to run up in dat, pussy," he adjusted his massive erection in his pants. My eyes followed his movement of their own volition.

"But since you all ready to go and shit, Imma let yo uptight ass go chill wit your friends tonight. Just know this, Imma get dat pussay," he mashed the elevator button to start it moving again.

The doors to the elevator opened and as soon as they did, I flew past him. I almost ran smack into my friends, Trisha and Neiman. "Honey, we were just coming to look for you," Neiman was the first to speak.

"You alright, Harmony?" Trisha asked looking from me to Thug who was still standing in the elevator, his hand holding onto the door.

"Remember what I said Harmony. Imma be callin' ya soon. Make sure you answer the phone too, shit," he said and punched the button on the elevator for the doors to close.

"What was that all about, Harmony Fletcher? And you better not tell me nothing either. I saw how that fine ass young stud was checking you out," Trisha said knowingly.

"I have to agree with Trisha. He sure is fine." Neiman perked his mouth and agreed.

"You both are seeing things that aren't there," I said, lying. "I need a drink or three. Shit, somebody give me a drink. Let's get this party started," I said as I tried to wipe Thug and the kiss we just shared in the elevator far from my thoughts.

At least that's the plan, I thought unconvincingly to myself as I let the music and liquor carry me away. But the taste of his kiss still lingered on my lips and in my mouth. That nigga was Thuggalicious.

CHAPTER 9
THUG

The whole ride back down to the main floor felt like forever in time. In some odd, immature way, it seemed like I'd left something behind, when I left Harmony with her friends. Though the music was playing, my thoughts were vaguely interfering with me having a good time. I kind of missed shawty's smart ass mouth and that cool ass vibe already, the way she smiled, the soft tone in her voice, and the way she pronounced those words that seemingly floated from her lips. I knew I sounded crazy as fuck, but that's how a nigga was feeling as the elevator floor released the pressure and the doors slid opened.

"Damn, Thug, my nigga you looking good. When you get out? I saw your—" was all I heard. I didn't even bother to look back at the bitch; she wasn't no Harmony. It was hard to shake her, shake it or whatever it was we had just shared. I was still caught up in those brief moments I shared with shawty and I knew she could be more to me than just a fuck or a kiss. When our lips finally touched, I got hella shook. That shit felt like letting off a choppa and reloading dat bitch a second time. I felt so relieved from everything when I had her in my grasp. It's crazy cause, a nigga had just got out of jail and ran up on the most beautiful thing out-chea in these streets. Shawty ain no thottie, though. She is a real grown ass woman. I needed that. I needed a woman that played hardball like she did with me. I had never felt so alive before. Harmony released all the bullshit that was really bugging a nigga. She made me feel some type of way and I knew I could be better her than whoever that lame ass nigga was that broke her heart. I just needed more time with her so I could show her.

"Aye, my nigga, I got dat loud pack, fuck with me," I said to a random nigga who was standing on the wall. The nigga didn't act like he was trying to cop, so I kept it moving. Thug ain't have no time to waste.

I found an empty seat in a corner booth and sat down. This would be my chill spot for the night, all I would do was catch a few niggas as they walked by and sell a little weed.

I pulled out about a gram and dumped it on the table when I suddenly realized I didn't have no rillo. I'd left that shit on the counter at the store.

"Damn." It was silly as fuck, but my first impulse was to hit shawty up see if she had one; shid wasn't no store around this motherfucker.

I'll catch up with you two in a minute. Will that be a problem? I thought about how smooth those words slid of her sexy ass lips, the ones I'd just caressed with mine. I could eat that bitch booty, ain lying.

The way shawty gasped for me and called my name in the elevator when I backed that ass up against the wall was turning me the fuck on. I laid the mac down on her and it seemed like she liked it just a little, but on the real, I couldn't tell behind those dreamy glares. I remembered how the features in her face were at that moment, those soft fuck me eyes, and surrendering wet lips. I wanted to fuck her mouth. The way I felt, I could have taken shawty in the bathroom and ate her out on the bathroom sink. Shid, I don't give a fuck, but it seemed like she did. The more I thought about it, the more it seemed like she was hesitant. In my moments of admiration for shawty, I suddenly remembered that I was the one doing all the talking, not her.

I don't wanna talk about it anymore, by the way how old are you? Her words played back and I suddenly remembered more reasons to think otherwise, like the way she pulled away from me at the door,

49

and the way shawty acted in a hurry to get back to her damn friends. It seemed like she was constantly shutting me down. I don't know about shawty, maybe she too stuck up for a nigga. Maybe she wanted some old dude who can tell her he'll be home right after his client leaves his office. Shid, maybe Harmony wanted a lawyer or a doctor, some shit like dat.

Damn, nigga, it was only a kiss.

After I thought about it, I was acting petty as fuck over this bitch and Thug don't need that shit. If shawty wanted a nigga, she would be with me right now at this table, but instead she was up there with her boozie ass friends sharing martinis and laughing her ass off. Harmony wasn't thinking about me at all. Thug from the hood and only hood bitches gone fuck with me. Maybe all I needed to do was keep it a hunnad and just stick to my trap queens. I needed to forget all about Harmony and stick to getting that paper was all a nigga really needed to be focused on, so I stood up and I took out my phone, scrolled down to that boozie bitch number and deleted that motherfucker, deuces.

CHAPTER 10
THUG

The next day was Saturday, so Bree was sleeping in, but I was already sitting on Gator front porch with the choppa on the stool and his celly in my hand. I had hollered at a few niggas last night at the club so that shit was gonna travel around. Niggas talk that plug talk like bitches talk about they hair-doo, who got the best shit and where you can get it from. I had already broken a pound down, most of it into all grams and the way these prices go up on loud, that was gone bring me stupid numbers so I knew I was bout to make hella cash. If a nigga wanted more weight, I would bust down a second pound and throw it on the scales and handle that shit.

"Damn sunny that a motherfucker out hea." I rubbed the sweat on my face and thought about how good big ass class of Kool Aid or Faygo pop would be. If you ever came to da souf in the summer time, you already knew how hot it could be in Atl. I took off my tee and paced it on the chair.

"Damn, you up early." I looked back to see Bree standing in the door with her panties and bra on.

"Man, cover that shit up. Don't nobody wanna see yo lil ass tits and shit." I placed my hand over my mouth like I was about to fucking throw up.

"Thug, ion know why you be acting like that with me damn, all the shit I done did for you."

"Wha? Bruh, you ain't never did shit for me," I replied.

"Well, what's this?" she pulled a greenish block wrapped in Saran Wrap from behind her back. I took my hand away from my mouth.

"That's my shit? I knew I left it over here. It was under…"

"The loose brick under the porch. I know, boy. I pay attention to everything you do, nigga," she said rolling her neck and eyes as I got up to retrieve my shit.

"Well, you can stop paying attention, shawty, cause it ain happening. Now give me my shit foe I go up top on yo ass. Shit, you almost made me snap on yo brother for nothing." I reached for the block, but she held it way out of reach and behind her back so that my arms were chasing it.

Our eyes were closer than they'd ever been. My chest was on hers when I heard a car pull into the yard. I glanced over my shoulder and noticed the car. It was a Honda Civic Coupe.

***

HARMONY

"Harmony, why did we have to come over here in this part of town just for some weed?" Trisha smacked her lips once we entered Bankhead.

"I had been begging Greg to put me on the guy he gets his weed from because he usually had that fire shit. Nobody knows Greg and I smoke. One day, I caught him smoking by the dumpsters at school and we been cool ever since. He usually got it for me from this guy Gator, but I think he's getting tired of me bugging him about it so he finally gave me the directions so that I could start getting it from Gator myself. He said the house was easy to find, to just to pull up and ask for Gator." She peered out the passenger side window and pressed her hand to her temple.

"Did you call his ass first to make sure it was okay? You know these motherfuckers over here will shoot your ass."

"Who, Gator?"

"Yes."

"No, I'm sure Greg told him I was coming, Trisha," I said

and hoped she would stop bugging the fuck out. She was making me nervous with that kind of talk. I hoped that when we pulled up, Gator would be posted up as Greg said he would. It would only take a few minutes to get it and we would be gone, or at least I hoped we would. "Chill out, Trisha. It won't take but a minute for us to swing by this guy Gator's house and get a quarter bag. If you guys hadn't smoked up my shit last night, I would still have some. I'm just going over here to get a little bit, not much. This will last me a few more days," I assured her. "See? We already here, It's the third house on the left. That's it right there." I indicated a white house with a porch and black shutters around the windows.

I eased to a stop and put my car in park to peer at the house in question. My mouth dropped open when I saw a familiar figure on the front porch, but what stumped me all the more was when I saw the familiar figure tussle with a scantily clad young woman. He was shirtless and his jeans hung low on his hips. His shoulders were wide and his abs were ripped with several tats.

"What's wrong with you?" Trisha glanced my way as I looked at Thug and his girlfriend make out without shame on the front porch. *Damn, I knew it! All these niggas are full of shit.*

"Girl, that's Thug. You remember the guy I was talking to at Club Sapphire last night?" My mouth tightened with disappointment when I thought about that passionate kiss we shared and his promise to call me afterwards, knowing the whole time he had a damn girl. *He's such a liar, just like all the other men that I had dealt with in the past.*

"That sure is him. He must be a friend of Gator's or something because he sold you some the other day, right?" she asked me.

"Yeah," I replied feeling some type of way. "Let me go get this weed so we can get the hell out of here. You don't even have to get out. You just hang tight right here. I won't be but a minute," I promised and slammed the car door.

"Excuse me, but I need some tree."

Thug's eyes grew to the size of two half dollars. "Bruh, what you doing out here?"

"Do I look like a man to you?" I asked, as sarcasm dripped from my voice. "I'm not your bruh and I just told you," I rolled my eyes.

"Git off me, Bree," Thug pushed her away.

I guess he had her trained, because the little thot took a seat and didn't say anything else. She just sat there and sucked air between her teeth and stared hard at me. I turned my head and glared back at Thug.

"Damn, okay, but what the fuck you tripping foe?" He finally stepped away from the girl and rocked his shoulders as he came closer to the edge of the porch. He had one hand securing the front of his pants so they wouldn't fall. He looked at me with a crazy ass look on his face.

"All I want is some tree," I reiterated once again. I just wanted to get my shit and get the hell away from Thug and his girlfriend.

"Aye, this some different shyt though. It's that loud pack, so it's gone cost you a little more," he said and the wrinkles withered slowly from above his eyes. "I tell you what, Imma just give you this right here for the same price as the mid, but don't be telling nobody that shit." He handed me the weed and I shoved the money into his hand.

"I don't need you to be doing me any favors." I had gotten so pissed, that I'd forgotten to ask where the main man Gator was. I just walked back to my car instead. I placed the weed in the console and took out my phone. I scrolled down found the name Thuggalicious. I deleted his number and dismissed his ass.

"You okay, girl?" Trisha's voice floated to me. Her tone was low and sympathetic.

"Yea girl." I started the car and noticed Thug standing by the driver's side window.

I didn't even look into his face, I just talked out the side of my mouth uncaringly about him being a two-bit player who didn't know squat about how to treat a real woman like me. But he didn't leave even though I continued to ignore him. Finally, I turned my eyes his way and met his simmering glare.

"What?" I asked but Thug didn't say shit, he just stood there. I could feel his eyes on me though.

"You know he heard everything you said, right?" Trisha whispered.

For some reason, I felt this shallow emotion that wouldn't let me sink Thug into my deepest sea of forgetfulness. As something inside forged me, I looked at Thug and his eyes met mine through the window. It was cracked. My eyes got big and round at the thought of him hearing me.

Damn! Embarrassment spread all over me. I hurried and reached for the electronic button to slide my tinted window back up so he couldn't look into my angry face. *Slick ass motherfucker.* He was nothing but a two-bit player, just as I thought. I fumed inwardly at my weakness of even giving him the time of day in the first place. Again I looked away. I made myself look straight ahead so I wouldn't have to look into his lying ass face ever again.

I let down my sun visor to look at myself in the mirror attached to the back of it. My hair was pulled back into a simple ponytail. Wisps of my soft hair curled at my edges. *I could use a little edge control later.* I took my hand to smooth back the stray wisps of hair. I looked down at the hot pink tank top I had on with a pair of daisy duke shorts. My feet were encased in flat strappy sandals. My freshly pedicured fuchsia painted toenails complemented my tank top. I looked at everything that I could instead of him and just as I was looking elsewhere, the back door suddenly open and closed.

Shit! Why hadn't I thought to lock my doors?

"That beauty ain't going nowhere. Aye, homeguh, let me catch that front seat foe a sec. Here and take Ms. Harmony out to eat or some of that girly shit y'all do after y'all leave here." I looked in the mirror to see him sitting in my back seat. Thug held out a wad of cash and gave it to her. Trisha took one look at the money and got the hell out.

"Oh wow, no prob. I'll be waiting on the porch," she said and took off before I could stop her betraying ass. Thug got in the front seat.

"Aye, you," he said. When I wouldn't look that way, he added, "Shawty? Stop flexin," in a raspy southern accent that sounded so cocky. I flinched when I felt his fingers sliding across my bare skinned thigh.

"Excuse you!" I slapped his hand away. How dare he touch me after having his hands all over another woman just minutes before? Thug had a smug expression on his face as his eyes seemed to eat me alive. I let my sun visor flap back up and glared at him. "Get the hell out of my car," I said, but Thug paid me no mind, he just sat back and made himself comfortable in my car.

I placed my hand on the steering wheel and perked my lips. I was not hearing the lame ass excuses, not this time. Thug's eyes raked over my body but lingered on my brown legs. "What bring you to my side of town anyways? I know it wasn't just to get no weed?" He asked me with a smirk on his handsome face.

He had some nerve to come up here in my car and try to make light conversation with me and shit. I looked through my window and didn't see Trisha or Thug's girlfriend on the porch.

"Yes, I did just come over to get some weed, but I thought some guy named Gator lived here. Where is Trisha and where is your girlfriend?" I questioned him and folded my arms across my chest.

"Oh, he ain't here. What girlfriend?" he returned with a

question of his own.

"Oh, so you're going to try and play me about what I witnessed when Trisha and I drove up. You and your little girlfriend was making out in broad daylight for anyone to see," I said letting my attitude get the best of me.

"Damn, ma! I know yo ass don't think that Bree my girlfriend. That's Gator's little sister, shid! Bree like a sister to me. Ion never looked at her like dat. We just cool," he said gazing into my eyes sincerely.

I looked away from him, because I knew he was lying and I didn't want him to see the look in my eyes. It would surely give away how upset I really was about seeing his arms around somebody other than myself.

"Bae, look at me," he said putting a hand under my chin, navigating me towards his convincing gaze, but I had something waiting behind my lips when he did.

"You're lying. I don't prance around in my underwear in front of my brother like she did with you, and my brother's hands don't be all over me like yours were on her either. What kind of fool do you take me for, Thug?" I tried to jerk my face from his grasp, but he held me firmly him, making me look at him.

"Shid, fuck it then, let's go."

"Go where?"

"Anywhere bae. If that's my bitch inside, why the fuck would I get in the car with yo ass and leave? So come on start the motherfucking car. Let's go."

"Thug, you're lying." I placed my hand to my forehead and blew a frustrated sigh. I had gone through this type of shit before with Byron.

"I've never lied to you, bae, and I don't preciate you sayin' I did either," he stated with heat entering his own eyes. "Tell me one thang dat I lied to you bout?" He continued to hold my chin and give me the stare down.

"Well, if you're not lying to me about this girl, then you lied about calling me. Why would you ask for my cell number if you never had any attention of calling me? Not that it bothered me or anything," I quickly added, before I slapped his hand away from my face.

"Oh, it don't bother you? Dafuq!" He jerked back and stared at me with those eyes. "And why dafuq you hit me, shawty? You right, I didn't call. My bad, I was feeling some type of way. It juh seem like fo a minute you ain really wanna fuck with a nigga. You could have chilled with me a little while longer at the club, but you made a nigga feel like you couldn't wait shake me so you could get back to yo friends and shit. I usually don't even give a fuck about no broad, but you just seem different," he admitted.

I sat back in my seat to see if he was serious. I looked over at him. Thug's expression didn't let on if he was truly trying to play me or not. "You said you had business to take care of first, remember?" I questioned him.

"Yeah I remember, but that was before we got caught up in dat steamy as fuck kiss, bae. Got damn, shawty, you had a nigga all caught up and I wuz mo than ready to whip this dick on yo pussy, the way yo ass was grinding all up on me and shit made me almost forget about what it was I had to handle," he said cupping his crotch.

My eyes traveled down to his hand movement. I could see his erection lengthening and stretching right before my very eyes. It looked like a got damn radiator hose in his pants. "Well, I was just letting you handle whatever it was you had to handle."

"Nah, ain handle what I really should've handled. See what yo juicy ass do to a nigga?" He said as he eyeballed me from the tip of my head to my fuchsia painted toenails. "I can see it in those sexy eyes of yours. Yeah you wanna fuck too."

"I don't," I said, but before I could even finish my sentence, he reached over and slid his hand down the waistband of my shorts. It happened so fast that I didn't try to stop him.

"Oh, so your pussy just wet for nothing?" he asked as he slipped his finger through the center of my folds and then strummed a finger against my clit.

"Stop it! Mmm," my head fell back against my headrest as I squeezed my thighs tightly together. A heat of reluctance ran through me. My movement had left his hand trapped tightly between my legs. I would need to just get Trisha and get the hell out of Bankhead.

"That's it, babe. Grind the shit outta my hand. Show me how you do on a dick," he directed and continued to caress my pussy with the tip of his finger. The more I squeezed, the better it felt. It was a losing battle that I wasn't ready for.

I couldn't believe that in broad daylight, I was in my car letting a guy I'd just met finger me off. I tried clinching down again, hoping to free myself from him, but it only sent another feel-good tingle all over me. His fingers dipped in and out faster and faster inside of my saturated heat rebelliously. I could feel the throbbing inside of my slick walls increase from his manipulation. I was about to cum.

My breasts swelled and my nipples hardened. A car passed by, but I was too far gone to pay it any attention as I rode Thug's hand. All of those feelings of fury had gone some place to the back of my mind. Instead, the fury landed in the center of my core and readied to burst forth like a dam all over his hand. For the next few minutes, he didn't even say shit. He just watched me squirm to his authoritative command. Just knowing that he was watching me get off had my pussy thumping like crazy.

Thug reached over with his other hand and slid it under my pink tank top to cup one of my bare breasts. I made a slight whimpering sound when he twirled my nipple between his thumb

59

and forefinger and fingered me at the same time. He played with my pussy until he found that spot to make me shiver and he stayed right there on it. I held on to the steering wheel and panted in short passionate breaths.

"I'm cumming, Thug," I cried out in pleasure as an electrical shock zinged through my core and swept down to release my sticky nectar. I was greedy as I continued to hump his hand and I exhaled on a passion filled sigh.

"You're so fuckin' hot when you cum, Miss Lady. This my pussy and you better not give it away to nobody." Hearing him tell me that it was his had me turned on. I couldn't even lie and when he told me I better not let anyone else have it, I got insanely aroused…even more than I already was if that was possible. My juices ran free onto his fingers and hand and I started humping his still plunging finger back again.

The front door slammed and both of our eyes flew towards the house. Trisha and the girl named Bree were back out on the porch. I had lost all perspective in the time or where I was. Thug's hand slid from under my shirt and out of my shorts. He brought his sticky fingers coated with my pussy juices to his mouth and licked off my juices.

"Dat pussy taste juh like motherfucking sweet water," he mumbled.

My body craved for him more than it had ever craved for anyone else in that moment. I wanted his dick deep inside of me. I needed it deep inside of my swollen pulsating pussy.

"Gimme yo number again," he said.

"No," I replied as if I didn't want him to have it. I shook my head.

"Stop playin'…I wanna take you out," he stated.

"Maybe you do, but I'm not giving it to you again. Hey," I shouted when he picked up my cell phone and pressed some digits in it before he hit send to make a call. He then laid my cell phone back down where he found it.

"I'll be callin' you soon. On the real dis time," he said and got out of the car and slammed my door.

Trisha came bounding down the stairs and ran over to the car. Thug held the car door open for her until she got inside.

"Thanks, Trisha, I owe you one," he said and closed the door once she was in. My panties were soaking wet and I needed to get home quick. I hurriedly started my ignition and drove off without even a goodbye.

"You do know what kind of friend you are, right?" I asked glancing over at her.

"Yeah, the best kind you could ever wish for," she replied teasingly.

"You think so, huh? Traitor," I said and frowned at her.

"At least I got this wad of cash to blow on us a high price meal," she replied and took the wad of cash from her purse to show off. "Besides you know you feenin' for that young fine ass nigga. You a cougar." Trisha laughed aloud.

She didn't know how right she was, but I wasn't ready to divulge that kind of information at the present moment. "Humph," I said instead and shook my head in denial. I drove in silence with Thug and what he did to me heavily on my mind. My pussy was still singing from his Thuggalicious touch.

CHAPTER 11
HARMONY

"Harmony!" I suddenly became aware of my brother Markus's fingers snapping in my face as he tried to gain my attention. "What's wrong with you? I've called your name three times," he said as he took another bite of his burger. We were having dinner at one of our favorite eateries, but my mind was somewhere else.

"I'm so sorry, Markus. What did you say?" I asked, looking into his eyes which held the same bluish hue as my own.

"I asked what's been going on with you, little sis. I'm sorry I've been real busy lately and haven't been able to check up on you as much as I would like to," he said acting like the protective older brother that he had always been.

"Not much. I've been working and going shopping, you know that sort of thing. Mostly, I go to the movies with Trisha or catch something off Netflix," I replied and took a bite of my own. I swallowed a mouth full and dipped a fry in some ketchup. "Other than that, I'm pretty much home grading papers and preparing my lesson plans."

"You aren't dating anyone new since you broke up with Byron are you?" he inquired with a sharp scrutinizing gaze.

"No," I answered him and bit into my Swiss mushroom burger. "Are you going to eat those fries?"

"Here." He passed the plate and I raked some off onto mine.

"Byron seemed like a nice enough guy," he said and wiped his face with a napkin. "Even though I wasn't around him much. You never did tell me what happened between the two of you."

Markus didn't know how wrong he was about Byron being a nice guy. Maybe I should have brought him around my brother

62

more. Maybe Markus could have picked up some bad vibes about him and warned me. I would never say those words aloud so I said instead, "Am I supposed to tell you every little detail of my life, Markus?" I placed the burger on the plate and looked my brother right in the face. "I'm a grown woman and you need to start treating me as such,"

"I'm sorry, Harmony, but since mom and dad died in that car wreck when you were seventeen, I've just felt it's been my responsibility to look out for my younger sister. You are the only thing I have of value in my life."

"I'm sorry, Markus," I said feeling repentant. "I know you mean well and I really appreciate all that you have done and do for me. You are the greatest brother a sister could ever ask for. I just wish you'd lighten up a bit and not worry so much about me. I made it fine to this point and I will continue doing so." I tried to convince him. "Besides, isn't it time you found a woman, maybe start dating and give me a couple of nieces and nephews?" I asked him.

"I really don't have time to date or take anyone seriously right now. A woman would never understand my grueling schedule."

"Have you even given anyone a chance to?" I asked him. My cell phone rang and *Thuggalicious* appeared on the screen. "Ah, hold that thought, Markus, I need to take this call," I held up a finger and put the phone to my ear. "Hello?"

"Hello? Man don't be helloing me. When you see daddy calling you betta find another word in the vocabulary, Ms. Fletcher, how bout 'bae'?" I switched the phone to my other ear and opened my mouth to say something when suddenly I noticed Markus staring with those overly protective eyes.

"You're absolutely right."

"Are you okay?" Markus intruded and I gave him a nod, but a raspy muffled tone rattled my eardrum.

"Who the fuck is dat? Sound like a nigga to me," Thug said.

"It's my brother."

"Bruh my ass. Ahite, bruh, imma need to meet that nigga. When imma meet him?" I swallowed deeply.

"Oh, soon. Look, I have to go. I'll call you back."

"Yea, whatever. Tell Bruh Thug said, 'what's han'nan'."

"Will do."

"Oh, yeah, it was something else I was gone tell you."

"What's that?"

"I miss you, boo." There was a slight pause from my end of the phone. For a second, my mind just simply went blank. I couldn't call him no boo, bae or none of that stuff, especially not in front of Markus.

"Well," I started thinking of something to say when the doors to the small burger joint opened and several guys walked through the door wearing dark colored tees and baggy jeans that were hanging off their asses.

The one in front caught my attention most. My eyes automatically responded and with it came along this awful flutter in my belly as our eyes collided. Damn, it was Thug.

"Well, what? Hello?"

CHAPTER 12
THUG

Bae look like she seen a got damn ghost or some. Ain even know she was here. Shid, her car wasn't parked outside, only a few random shits and onetime. I noticed twelve had an unmarked Crown Vic parked out there, but we been doing this shit right up under they nose for years. That's the name of the game, so on the real, I didn't even sweat it.

"Imma catch up with y'all in a min, bruh." I pulled up my pants up slightly and walked over to where Bae and where this nigga was sitting. The nigga was eyeing me before I could even get up on the table good.

"Shid, what's han'nan? You looking at me like you lost some." I rested my hand on the pistol that was in my draws.

"Thug, this is," Harmony stood, but I didn't even look her way for real.

"Aye, bruh can talk. That nigga got a mouth, don't he? Let him speak for himself."

"Excuse me, who the hell are you?" Markus asked none too nicely.

"Shid, I'm Thug, Zone 1 Bankhead. The Bluff all dat. Who you is, pah'tna?"

"Ah, excuse us, Markus. I just need to ah…Well, he and I need to talk for a quick second, Be right back." Harmony grabbed me like a boss bitch and shoved me to the side, her nails digging deeply into my chest as she snatched me by the collar. With a grim mug, I glanced down at her motherfucking hand and met a feisty ass mug that matched mine. *Damn, she a boss bitch.* I had found my match.

As her hands slid down my tee, I thought about how brave

65

and gangsta she was to even put her mu'fuckan hands on a nigga like me. Harmony knew I could beat the fuck outta her, but li'l momma didn't even give a fuck. She had heart and I liked that feisty shit.

"Come on. Now," she said in the most serious tone I'd heard her use since we had met. I could tell she was pissed the fuck off at me.

Um hum, bitch, I like when you mad. I pulled up my jeans and followed her sexy ass to the back. As we walked, I kept looking down at that duke. Shawty was strutting so fast that she could have broken the seams out them leggings she had on. Bitch looked like a horse from the back. We entered a small hallway and I continued to follow Harmony, mostly glancing at my celly, but also at that ass. Her large curves created something that was very irresistible. There's nothing like seeing a strong, black woman mad and in control. She opened the door to the women's restroom and pulled me by the arm.

"Bring your ass in here right now," she said and turned to face me. Her neck arched until she was looking me directly in my eyes. Time seemed to stall at that moment. Even when she was mad, shawty was fine as hell. Seeing that flare of frustration swimming in her eyes had me gone. She never wavered from my gaze and that sent a rush of adrenaline all through me. I wanted to just put her lil fine ass on top of the sink and eat her pussy and smell her duke just to say "I'm sorry." I knew I could get out of hand sometimes and shit like that, but I just lost it when I thought Harmony was going to fuck around with another nigga. Even though I knew the reason, I couldn't tell her that.

"What the hell is wrong with you? You're acting like a nut out there. You can't be running around with your pants all off your butt in public and talking that trap talk shit to everyone like you just don't care."

Who da fuck she talkin' too in dat tone of voice?

"I don't," I said looking the other way and shit.

66

"You don't what? You don't care, Thug? You don't care about life or me or us?" She grabbed me again, this time pressing her finger into my chest.

When Harmony's lips released those words, I felt like I had just fallen off a got damn cliff or something. Shawty had a way to say shit to make a nigga really look at shit in a different way. I knew one thang, though it was no way in hell that a nigga could say he ain care about those soft and plump pink lips, or the way she handled me. I tried like hell to look in her eyes, but I just couldn't so I looked the other way again.

"No, look at me!" Harmony reached up courageously and grabbed the side of my chin and, even though I hate to admit it, a nigga felt some type of way about looking into those innocent sky blue eyes. She also had a nigga hard as a damn boulder and ready to release a massive load inside of her mouth or ass, whichever one I could get inside first, but I knew she was too pissed for that lovely dove shit.

CHAPTER 13
HARMONY

"Why the hell you looking at me like that?" I said as the sudden look in his eyes changed from tolerance to a sultry drunken gaze that ignited my flesh wherever his hazel eyes lingered for long.

"Like wat, Shawty?" he said licking his lips sexily. I saw that quick flash of something in him as he hid those emotions behind his gaze, but I would handle his ass later because Markus was waiting.

"I really need to get back to my brother before he come looking for me," I said backing away towards the restroom door, but Thug was faster than me and he cut me off and locked the bathroom door. The sound of the lock sounded loud in the airy restroom, almost echoing.

"Nigga, I ain wor bout' yo punk ass brother. You stepped to a nigga in here all fied up and shit. I hear wat yo sayin' and all, bae, but shid, I'm Thug and Imma be Thug all day. Ain't no motherfucker finna stop me from being me. I ain no doctor, lawyer or none of those other professionals that you used to dealing with. If you want a nigga to do betta, Imma need some type of incentive," he said backing me up against the sink.

"Wha—" I tried to get out when my eyes slid down to the zippered area of his baggy jeans. He unzipped his jeans and pulled out what I desired the most and made it jump for me.

"Yeah, you see wat yo fine ass always doin' to me. Yo juicy ass keep me hard as fuck! Tell me you don't want none of this."

"Thug, I need to get back to my brother, so stop playing," I replied as my nipples hardened under my clingy halter top. I couldn't take my eyes off his gigantic dick.

"Nah, I ain playin'. I came up here in dis piece to eat. You wouldn't let a nigga get no burger. You had to flex on me and shit, brought me back here in the women's bathroom, so that's jus wat imma do. I'mma get me something to eat and right now ion want no motherfucking burger," he said licking his lips in that sexy way of his again. "I got a taste fo me sum sushi!"

My breath caught in my chest when he gripped me around the waist and pulled me to his chest. *Was he going to take it, right here, right now?* Thug claimed his first kiss since the last time we had seen each other. Our mouths clammed together and smacked as he thrusted his delicious, hot tongue into my mouth. His kiss was just as delicious as the last time. With my pussy jumping for him, my mouth greedily received his tongue like he was the precious air that I needed to breathe. The smell of his cologne enveloped my senses as his tongue swirled and tangled with my own. I groaned between the onslaught of his simmering hot kisses. The sensations in my pussy began to awaken and stir with a need of its own.

"Shid, baby," he murmured hotly against my lips and I placed my hands on his shoulders. "All I been thinkin' bout is tasting that sweet pussy of yo's ever since you bussed a nut on my hand in the car. I've been thirsty for a taste of my puss ever since. You do kno this puss belong to me now, right?"

The words that slid off his tongue caused my emotions to run havoc with the thought of his mouth and tongue inside me so intimately. I knew he really wanted to eat my pussy, but right then wasn't the place or time and that's what made it so hard. My heartrate increased when I felt one arm come around to push my halter top up to reveal my bare full round breasts to his hot gaze.

"I ain't never seen a titty so gorgeous," he exclaimed. "Let me suck it just once. One time and I promise I'll stop," he said leaning in to cup one breast in his hands. I wanted to say something, but all of my words were stuck as his head bent down and took one rigid brown nipple greedily into his mouth and sucked.

"Sss, Shit," I sighed aloud as his tongue slid around my areola before taking my full nipple into his mouth to tantalize and titillate with his tongue.

"Can I taste your pussy one time too, just once?" he asked me with a deeper voice that was filled with desire.

"Yes," I said softly as lust overwhelmed me and led me to do something that was so forbiddingly dangerous and left me with no recourse, but to let him do whatever he wanted with me. I willingly became his for the taking.

But before I would let him do it, I would need one more feel of that mouth against mine. My hands reached under his shirt to do what they had been itching to do since laying eyes on his muscular back and ripped six pack abs. I took off his shirt and threw it on the floor.

His mouth captured mine again which caused my juices to stir even more to a foamy concoction inside my leggings. My hands stroked over his back as I gave myself over to the kiss in every way. It was just him and me and no one else dared to intrude on our intimate moment.

I burned inside with heated anticipated lusty thoughts of how it would feel once he licked me. I felt his hands hook under the waistband of my leggings and slide them down. He did this without breaking our kiss. Finally, after a while his lips released mine. My lips were moist and dewy and well kissed as my chest heaved up and down in a rhythmic fashion.

"You a freaky lil hoe. Damn, baby!" He stepped back and noticed for the first time that I didn't have on any panties. He licked his lips again before finally looking back up into my eyes. "I can't wait to taste that pretty pussy and it's shaved too, just like I like it," he said and lifted me by my waist. He positioned my bare ass on top of the sink. He removed my heels and placed my foot in his mouth and I closed my eyes and melted at the warm sensation. He finished

70

pulling off my leggings until they were completely off.

He urged my ass to the edge of the sink's countertop before he bent to come face to face with the object of his desire. I leaned back on my elbows and spread my slippery folds open for him. When he leaned in, I closed my eyes at the first swipe of his tongue against my protruding clit and he began his feast.

"Shid, dese pussy lips phat as fuck and juicy too," his voice vibrated against the plumpness of my slick pussy. I held back a moan and bit down on my lip. With a greedy stride, he kissed and licked at my wet lips before attacking my clit again with his thick hot tongue. He began slapping the stem of my clit with his tongue repeatedly until I became numb with pleasure.

"I'm going to cum for you soon, don't stop," I cried out as my pussy quivered and vibrated under his mouth. One of my hands went to his head as he spread my thighs even further apart which left me wide open and vulnerable to his assault. His whole mouth cupped around my entire slit. He pushed his tongue deep inside me and tongue fucked me like it was his dick. "Ah shit, Thug," I cried out and pushed him deeper. "Please don't stop," I begged as his tongue swirled deliciously on the inside of my hot walls.

My hips moved with conjunction with his deep tongue strokes. Damn, it had been a while since I had felt this good. Hell, if I had to admit the truth, this was the best oral that I had ever received in my life. I looked down at Thug eating me out. He was going down on me like the ultimate connoisseur leaving no nook or cranny untouched.

My toes started to curl as the throbbing of my pussy intensified. Every swipe and lick from his tongue was bringing me closer to the edge. "Tell daddy who dis pussy is," he demanded looking up at me with my nectar glossing his lips.

"This is your pussy," I let out a whimper when he slid a finger into my hot spot and curved it at an angle. He touched a spot with his finger movement that caused my eyes to roll back in my head. My legs begin to tremble and I humped against his face in uncontrollable abandon.

"If dis is my pussy cum for daddy," he demanded before diving his head back between my thighs. I attempted to squeeze my thighs on either side of his, head but he forced my legs back wide open to his attack.

"Sssss, ahhhhh, damn it, fuck it to hell!" I cried out in ecstasy. "I'm cumming, daddy! I'm cumming," I whaled out in succession. My orgasm rumbled to the forefront and spilled over like a tide as I squirted my essence into his mouth.

Thug could be heard lapping at my juices and moaning his pleasure to be on the receiving end of my offering. "Anybody in here?" A loud knock sounded at the door, but I was already having my next orgasm.

I humped faster towards his licks until I caught it and released with the rhythm of his licks. When I had gotten it all out, I nearly jumped out of my skin and my cheeks flushed against my brown skin as I realized what I had just allowed to happen.

"Tell her you're going to be a while," Thug said as he reached for my leggings to help me put them back on. I did as he suggested and avoided his eyes as I turned to the mirror to make sure everything was in place.

"Look at me, Harmony," Thug said, placing his shirt over his head.

I looked down to avoid his eyes staring at me in the mirror. When it was on him, he gently touched my shoulders to turn me around to face him. "You do know there is no going back between you and me." I put my clothes back on.

"This shouldn't have happened. We shouldn't have even happened. This is all just too much for me I'm not ready for this," I said softly as my senses returned.

72

"Feel this right chere. You can keep fucking playing like you don't want it and Imma show you just how much you do," he replied with my hand wrapped around his huge erection. "When I whip dis dick out on yo ass you betta be ready fo it. I'm not braggin' or nuthin, but yo ass betta be able to take all of it too," he said before he released my hand and placed another searing kiss on my lips. His tongue thrusted into mine and swirled until he was satisfied. I could taste myself on his tongue.

"Dats how sweet yo pussy taste. You feel me?"

"We got to get out of here. Let me see if the coast is clear," I said and hurried over to the door without answering his question. I unlocked the door and saw no one outside the door. "You go out first and then I will follow in a minute," I urged him.

"Our time is coming, Harmony." My name rolled off his tongue like sweet honey. "Bet dat," he said and winked at me. He adjusted his loose hanging jeans and left me standing alone, but completely satiated in the women's restroom.

I was in some deep shit with Thug and I was feeling more for him than I was willing to admit. "What in the hell have you gotten yourself into Harmony Fletcher?" I said before exiting the restroom with Thug heavy on my mind as always. Damn, I think I need a thug.

CHAPTER 14
THUG

"Yeah okay but what should yo punishment be though." I looked down into those baby blue eyes and traced the word love around her lips. Damn you fine as hell. Lips looking like a set of pussy lips. I want your mouth and yo pussy at the same damn time. As my inches stretched and spread in my jeans, I stood there thinking about what I would do to this feisty motherfucker.

"Whatchu wanna do, Thug?" She shrugged uncaringly. I looked at the way her gaze never changed. It was something about this older woman that I couldn't get enough of. Shawty was standing her ground and I liked it.

"So you think it's cool to just grab Thug and slang him in the bathroom like you running shit? You just gone show yo little ass off in public and think I'm not gone do shit about it? Huh?" I walked closer and paced around her in dominant circles. Harmony crossed her arms like she wasn't about to bow down and smacked her lips.

"Tsk."

"Harmony, I'm not one of your little fifth grade students that you can just tell what to do. Turn yo ass around," I growled into her ear. Harmony repositioned her stance and stood there like rebellious teenager. I grabbed her by the wrist and curled it behind her back like the police do. I spun her ass around and made her face the bathroom sink. She blew a sigh as I shoved her hands forcefully in the direction of the sink.

"Grab that motherfucking sink. If you even flinch it's going to be worse on you." I threatened with a low, aggressive tone.

"Okay," she finally whimpered. Harmony placed both hands on the sides of the sink obediently and looked into the mirror. From behind I could see the reluctance on her face.

"Now, when I pull these pants down, Imma need for you to comply with me, Ms. Teacher. Got dat?" Harmony nodded and I kneeled behind her *and slid her leggings down to her mid thighs. I could smell her perfume and a whiff of that sweet pussy.*

I got harder instantly with anticipated thoughts of what it was going to feel like once I finally got a piece of that grown ass.

"Thug, I'm sorry." I coached her to say, but I only heard the smacking of her rebellious ass lips again. With a slow adoringly rub, I slid my nose over the curves of her ass and smelled every part of her like a got damn dog in heat. I buried my nose in the center of her ass and sniffed. The scent of a woman really turned me on. My anticipation accelerated above all rational thinking and I melted inside. Fucking shawty was one thang, but this shit was on a whole nother level. Harmony would learn to obey Thug and I would make sure of that.

As the blood in my veins pumped faster, filling the whole length of my manhood, I allowed her a few more seconds to submit.

"Thug, I'm sorry,' say it,"I mumbled, but Harmony was hardheaded, and she wouldn't say shit. I grabbed her thighs and pulled her body closer to my face. I slid my nose across the curves of her ass and stopped once again in the middle of her ass and smelled some more. The aroma of her perfume, pussy, and ass turned me on very badly. I wanted to fuck the shit out of Harmony like a motherfucker, but I wasn't going to make it easy.

With an unquenchable hunger for her love, I allowed my hands to finally peel her leggings down some, but I wouldn't take them off just yet. Her smooth skin brushed my nose slightly as she moved her ass to the side and my balls jumped in my jeans. It was in there, I knew it, that pussy was near. Somewhere behind those soft curves was the one thing that would get us both in some trouble. My dick rammed the front of my pants wanting so badly to get out, but I couldn't fall for her just yet. I spanked her on the ass.

"Thug, I'm sorry. I won't get up in your face no-more and act out I promise'. Say it, Harmony." Down on my knees, I mumbled, but still she was being a hard ass.

I ran my beard along her bare skin and let her energy flow through me. I became insanely greedy for her with her mean and stubborn ways. Every curve of her reminded me of what I couldn't have if she didn't comply with me. Shawty's ass was perfectly rounded and I really needed it. My eyes rode up and down the line in between her duke. It was more than I could resist. I stuck out my tongue and spread her cheeks apart with a wanting and desirous first lick.

*"Hello? Is someone in there? This is Marsha, the store manager."
Several times the lady outside the door knocked, but Harmony needed to know that when I tell her to do something, she better do it, so I didn't stop. I didn't stop licking up and down the crack of her ass.*

*"Sheila, see if you can find maintenance. I think this door's jammed."
Finally, the lady walked away. I traced some letters on the side of her ass. THUG. Just as I made the letter G, I heard Harmony's first words trying to break free. She was about to tell me she was sorry.*

"Okay, okay, you win," she said.

"Thug, I'm sorry," I threw back. The room grew silent again and shawty put her head back down disobediently. I stood up.

"Take them motherfuckers off right now got damit, take em off!" She unglued her hands from the sink and turned around to face me. She bent over to take off her leggings, but shawty wasn't too thrilled with it. I could tell. I grabbed her chin, but she moved her face from my grasp. Harmony stepped out of her shoes and took the leggings over her feet and I snatched them all and threw them across the room. I grabbed her by the back of her shoulder and thrust her the other way so that she was facing the sink again.

"Spread em," I snarled, prying my legs in between hers and spreading them further.

"Thug."

"Shut up!" I yelled and shoved my jeans down to my knees and pulled my dick through the slit of my boxers. "Now the next time I tell yo ass to say you sorry, you gone say it." I moved the fold of her pussy to the side with my thumb and ran this warm meat up in her. A large vein strained all the way down the side of her neck. Harmony arched her back and neck at the first thrust and grabbed the sink with all her might.

"Sss, not so," a moan tried to escape from her raspberry lips, but she withheld it defiantly. Looking in the mirror I could see the pain running to the

corners of her eyes as she squinted. I rammed her box with more dick. She jerked with the motion of my thrust. Her hair flung wildly down her back like a porn star who needed nothing more but to be dicked down real good. I stood on my tip toes and hit that corner "Walking yo sophisticated ass around here with all this good pussy don't wanna share with no-motherfucking-body. Scared to love and shit. Give it here got damnit." As my testicles tightened, I grabbed the arched curves of her waist and speeded up unsympathetically and pulled her towards my erection. "Got all dis good pussy and don't wanna share." I watched her mouth come open and another moan was swallowed as she bit down on the bottom of her lip as I pumped into her slippery circle.

I pulled out and dumped the first load on her ass and smeared it in with my dick. As it dissolved, I dipped my finger in it and stuck in on her pussy. I rubbed her clit several times and demanded that she cum for me. While doing so, my dick got hard and I put in back in. Over and over, our skins collided with forbidden lust. Harmony pressed her body to mine and began receiving the dick, but did so with a grudge. Pulling her waist into my length, I went faster, and started drilling that pussy until all you could her was the plucking sound. "Oh you wanna hold that shit in, huh? You ain feeling this dick Harmony?" I watched her facial expressions in the mirror, but she wouldn't moan for me. This bitch was being so hard. Harmony bit her lips to hold in every moan and that shit turned me on even more.

I picked her up and sat her on top of the sink facing me. For a minute, I just stood there jacking my meat and looking at her watch me do it. My second nut was coming. That shit turned me on to see her watching me. I had finally gotten a piece of Harmony. Her pussy juices were still on my dick and I mainly concentrated on that as she watched me. I looked in her disobedient eyes and dragged her thighs to the edge of the sink. An uncontrollable race of desire ran all over me. I shed all of my clothes and by then I could hear the voices of a woman and a man coming down the hallway one of which sounded like her brother.

"Don't stop, please." A willing gleam shot across her face as Harmony begged for more. She had finally decided she wanted some of Thug. There was

something interesting in her eyes as she squirmed in front of me and reached down to touch her pussy and rode the stem of her clit. She had already made two full circles when I heard the first knock. "Thug, please, please, please," Harmony reached out and held my head with both hands. She forced her tongue down my throat. I felt like I could have bussed from her kisses alone. Harmony sucked my bottom lip and pulled it wantonly and pushed away from me. When she did that, something inside of me gravitated towards her. I felt so compelled to give her the dick until she was satisfied, even if that meant getting caught. She looked sinfully good on top of that sink with her legs open and shit, begging for the dick.

Her eyes quickly filled with something sneaky behind them. Harmony blinked once and gnawed slightly at the inside of her cheeks. A kittenish smile sat and waited on her face as she pointed towards the bathroom stalls.

I licked my lips praising her erotic behavior and then Harmony's voice seemed to fade and her body slowly morphed into a fuzzy haze as she disappeared like a beautiful dream.

"Thug. Thug, wake up. I need you to take me to school," Bree said.

I sat up and found a wad of covers in my hand. "What the fuck?" I rubbed the sleep away from my eyes. Damn, today was Monday. I had forgotten I had to take Bree ass to school. I glanced to the left and saw a pillow turned sideways. I hope like hell a nigga wasn't humping that shit in my sleep.

"Word. Give me like two minutes to get myself together." I yarned. My dick was still on rock hard and I couldn't let Bree see that shit.

"Okay," she said softly and winked her eye as she closed the door.

CHAPTER 15
HARMONY

I closed my eyes and gave in to the pleasant sensations of Mitchell's strong capable hands on the back of my neck. After the week that I had, I really needed to treat myself to this massage at The Posh Spot. I was getting the whole nine yards done today. First, I started off with an aromatic soak, followed by the warm stone massage, facial, and waxing.

Now, Mitchell my most favorite masseuse in the world was ending my visit with a full body massage from my freshly pedicured nails down to my pedicured feet.

"You were very tense earlier, Miss Fletcher," Mitchell said as his hands slid down to my shoulders.

I was so relaxed by this point, that I wanted to doze off in a deep slumber. "Hmm," I murmured feeling more lose and relaxed than I had since the episode I had a week ago in the ladies' bathroom with Thug. I couldn't believe that we had been playing phone tag all week long. With testing going on all week long with my school's district, I had been extra busy with after school meetings.

"You mustn't stay away so long next time," Mitchell continued as the towel slid down further against my back. His fingertips slid under the soft cotton towel to massage my butt cheek.

I grunted aloud from the deep tissue massage. He slowly moved on to the next butt cheek and a smile bloomed on my lips as I thought about how it would feel if Mitchell's hands had been Thug's hands on my body. I surely wouldn't be lying still for sure.

"Thanks, Mitchell," I said when I was once again fully dressed. I tipped him handsomely for a job well done.

"Anytime, Miss Fletcher," said Mitchell as he gave me a

Colgate smile and a wink.

I easily returned his smile. Mitchell was a handsome, tall, and muscular white guy. But he wasn't my type. Another tall chocolate muscular body with tatts covering it deliciously came to mind as I made my way out the door to my car and drove home.

By the time I parked my car and walked up the stairs to my apartment door, my cell phone vibrated from inside of my handbag. I quickly removed it and glanced at my caller I.D. Thugalicious appeared on the screen.

"Hello," I spoke into the receiver.

"So we doing it like dat? Damn, okay, that's what's up, shawty." Thug's deep voice sent chills down my spine, the way he got an attitude with me for not calling him lately.

"I'm just getting home from the spa," I said inserting my key into my lock of my apartment door.

"Cool," he replied. There was a slight pause on the phone. Neither of us said anything. "Check this, ma. I have the crib to myself for a couple of hours. Swing by Gator's. I want to see ya."

I pulled my cell away from my ear and frowned before I replaced it against my ear. "Ahh, Thug, I don't think so. Why would I want to come and hang out at somebody else's crib when I got my own? You—"

"Dafuq? Oh you too boozie to come to the hood now?" His voice rose in anger as he cut me off.

"Thug, honestly, I wasn't trying to insult your intelligence or anything like that I just—"

"Whatever, bitch! I was jus tryin' to get wit yo ass but nah, yo sadity ass think you better than me is that what dis is, Harmony? You ain't the only fine motherfucker walking around Atlanta. I can fall off in some more pussy, don't get it twisted, shit," he stated without letting me get a word in edgewise.

"Thug! You took my words all wrong—" Silence was my

only reply when I realized that he had ended the call without even giving me a chance to explain myself fully.

"Damn it! What just happened here?" I said in the silence of my apartment. "I really need a smoke," I muttered before walking into my bedroom where I kept my stash. Well, what used to be my stash. Looked like I only had one rolled blunt left. I sat on the side of my bed and fired it up. There was only so many bitches that Thug was going to call me. I puffed several more times before I snuffed out the blunt to replace in the ashtray in my bottom drawer. This conversation needed to be handled face to face and then he could kiss my bitch ass for all I cared.

CHAPTER 16
HARMONY

There was an outside light on at Gator's when I parked my Honda Civic down some ways from his house. The front door was opened and I could see some people inside the house. I could see Thug's old school Chevy parked in the yard. I would have been here sooner but my brother called on my way out the door and I talked to him for at least thirty minutes before I drove over here to the other side of town.

Loud music could be heard coming from indoors. Thug hadn't told me that he had company when he invited me over about an hour ago. I walked slowly on the sidewalk leading up to the steps of Gator's house as the lyric's to Future's song "Trap Niggas" blasted at a high tempo through the house reaching outside into the streets.

Times getting hard but a nigga still gettin' it
Young rich niggas, in this motherfucker
When you wake up before you brush your teeth
You grab your strap, nigga
Only time you get down on your knees
Shooting craps, nigga

I walked the rest of the way up to the steps and peeked hesitantly through the open screen door. *Should I knock? Or should I just walk on in. I stood outside the door, feeling out of place and indecisive. I don't know the protocol for shit like this.*

"Whoa nie, Shawty," a voice said up behind me. "Yo fine ass must be lost or something."

My head swirled around to find myself a tall dark skinned

guy in faded sagging jeans and a Tupac shirt on. His feet were encased in a pair of Timberlands and several gold chains adorned his neck. He smiled to reveal a shiny gold grill and when my eyes traveled back to the top, I noticed he also had on a red bandanna and three tear drops tatted underneath his left eye.

"Ahh, I ah," I stuttered as he stared hard at me. The grimy look in his eyes made me shudder. It was hard to tell what this guy was thinking, but I was sure it was nothing pleasant. I thought about turning tail and running down the stairs back to my car, but I didn't come this far across town to see Thug just to leave before seeing him to tell him what was on my mind. "I'm looking for Thug," I finally got my words out.

"Oh Thug? He in the crib," he finally replied. "Come on, Shawty." He opened the screen door for me to walk in and beckoned for me. When I walked inside, he got behind me. "Umph…umph, shole got dat phat ass." The screen door slammed behind us and I looked back just in time to see the guy checking out my ass. "Yo! Anybody seen Thug?" His deep baritone voice floated over the loud music.

All eyes turned towards me as I stood there in my little yellow halter dress that stopped right above my knees. Some ratchet looking skanks were looking my way. "Oh…yea sure, he's upstairs in the second room on the left," One of the ratchets said with a slight giggle.

"Thanks," I said. I didn't know what their sly looks were all about and I didn't care. Maybe they were hating on the way I was dressed.

"You need any help finding yo way up there?" said the dude who walked me in.

'No, I think I can find it by myself," I replied, making my way through all the smoke floating around the room. With so much smoke, I would catch a high on top of a high by the time I got to my destination.

I walked up the short staircase and found the second room on the left easily enough. The door was closed but I could hear the sound of music coming from the room.

I knocked on the door lightly then slowly turned the knob. The door wasn't locked and the doorknob easily turned in my hands.

The bedroom was very dimly lit and my eyes took a moment to adjust to the dim lighting of the bedroom, but once they did and my vision was clearer, I walked further into the bedroom to find Thug sitting on the side of the bed. He had a cigar sized blunt hanging from between his lips. His head was hanging back with his eyes tightly closed. All of my senses just stopped and everything started to freeze in slow motion before my eyes. It was like my eyes were a camera taking in everything in slow motion. *Click…snap…click!*

Thug removed the cigar sized blunt from his mouth like he was Nino Brown and blew the smoke above his head. "That's what the fuck I'm talking bout, Nakita, take all of that dick, got damn that mouf game on fleek," he groaned out between clenched teeth.

My heart stopped beating for a moment in time. It was like the moon rose on a dark cloudy night, only to reveal peaks of light far and few between. My heart became captured in a whirlwind of horrid emotions as I stood there watching them.

Nakita, as Thug called her, seemed to have some good ass head. She had half of Thug's ten inches in her mouth and he was enjoying it. The second time I saw his dick had to be in another woman's mouth. Shit couldn't get any worse than this, or could it? So this is what he meant when he said pussy came easy for him.

Uncontrollable anger unlike it ever had before filled me as it began in the pit of my stomach to spew to my throat and eventually spilled from my lips. He wanted to be a player so be it, but from now on he wouldn't be worth my time after tonight.

Thug still hadn't noticed me as I stood there in the bedroom watching that skank assed bitch slobbering all over his huge dick. He was too busy enjoying himself. The way she was sucking it made me jealous as hell and livid at the same damn time.

"You bitch ass motherfucker you!" The bottle flew from my hand, but missed hitting Thug in his fucking head by a hair. I had picked up the first thing I saw, which was a beer bottle from off of a nearby dresser before I knew it. By that time both Thug and Nakita froze and looked up to find my presence in the room. Nakita released Thug's erection from her mouth and jumped to her feet. She tried to cover her breasts with her arms.

"What the fuck?" She looked at me with fright in her eyes.

"Damn, Bae! You tryna kill a nigga," Thug rose calmly from the bed and tucked his dick back inside of his baggy jeans and slid the zipper back in place. "When did you get here?" He asked with sluggish eyes. His voice was mellow and he wasn't feeling pain. But I was.

"Thug, go to hell!" My hands clenched at my sides. My hands itched to beat the shit out of him and bitch, too! It took everything in me not to go beat both of their no good, lowdown asses.

"Who the hell are you?" The bitch Nakita tried to grow some balls all of a sudden. She stepped back into her shorts and pulled a skimpy shirt over her braless breasts and walked over towards me.

"Bitch assed skank. You don't want none of this." I looked around and grabbed a second bottle off of the dresser. I stepped towards her without an ounce of hesitation.

"Aye Nakita, you can leave. I need to handle this shit with bae." Thug stepped between us as if he was protecting her.

"Da-fuck? You protecting your whores now, Thug? Did you even tell her you and I were seeing each other?" I shouted waving the bottle.

"Bitch, you don't know who you messin' wit," Nakita

shouted back and tried to reach for me over Thug's shoulder.

"Bitch, I wish you would!" Thug did an about face as he got in her face. "You touch my bae, and Imma lay yo ass the fuck down. Hoes come and go a dime a dozen, but it's only one lady in this room that I want," he said and placed his arm around my waist. "This my woman right chere and this shit ain't finna end over no side piece of pussy. You ain't gone be disrespecting this, not this right chere. Now get yo ass out like I said befo."

I looked at Thug as if he had spoken some kind of foreign language. He was crazy as hell talking about disrespect when he was the main one doing the disrespecting. I held up my hands, ready to wash my hands of both of their asses.

"I don't need this shit in my life right now. I'm better than this. Both of you can just have each other. No one need to leave on my account. By all means, I'll leave." The tears I had been desperately trying to hold back, came to the forefront and brimmed from my eyes.

"Hold on a minute, bae," I can explain," Thug said clasping my face between his hands.

Nakita stood back and looked on with a smirk on her ghetto ass looking face.

"Get your fucking pussy hands off of me!" I slapped his hands from my face. "You feeling all up in that bitch's pussy. How dare put your hands on me? I hate your fucking ass and don't ever try to contact me again." I backed out of the room with betrayal and hurt in my eyes.

"Let her go, Thug. You got me. I always will be here for yo ass like nobody ever will," said Nakita. "I'm yo ride or die chick. Always has been."

"Listen to your bad ride or die bitch, Thug. You two deserve to be together. Look like you both started from the bottom and still at the bottom," I said in a sarcastic tone to hurt him.

86

"You don't mean what you're sayin, Harmony. I fucked up okay, but I'm still the same nigga you couldn't get enough of. We had something special. Yo ass the one I want."

"Shut the fuck up," I screamed before turning and running down the stairs. I ran amidst the stares and the pain that ran rampant through my heart. I had gotten played by a young street thug by the name of Thug. I ran and ran as I tried to put distance between myself and him. Another set of footsteps could be heard behind me, but I continued to run as if my life depended on it.

I had my car door unlocked by the time I got to it with my electronic key chain. I opened my door and was almost safely inside when suddenly two hands grabbed me by my waist and lifted me out of the car. My mouth opened and let out a loud and angry scream.

CHAPTER 16
THUG

"Nigga, we ain't through discussing dis shit. Dafuq?" I said as I scooped her lil mean ass up out the car. Harmony grabbed my arms and squeezed until she had drawn blood.

"Like hell we are. Put me down, Thug."

"Ain doing shit and yo little ass claws feel like some baby ass ant bites. You can scratch me all you want, but yo ass fina come right the fuck back upstairs with me." I kicked the front door in and walked inside carrying Harmony inside.

"Everybody get the fuck out!" I growled and motherfuckers started scrambling to the door.

"Ain going nowhere." Bree rolled her neck and eyes.

"Bree take yo ass to yo room." By the time I made it upstairs everybody was gone. I kicked that door in too and tossed Harmony's ass on the bed.

"Let me tell yo ass some right now. You don't know shit about how I feel about you, girl. Yea…Shawty sucked my dick, but shid, that was only cause you was acting all boozie and shit. Your ass come buy weed from the hood, but you shole don't wanna come out hea to chill with a nigga." Harmony's gaze shifted.

"Thug, it's not even about coming out here to see you. You missed the whole fucking point. I was saying I shouldn't have to come to your homeboy's house to chill with you and,"

"That's what the fuck I just said."

"No let me finish. Shit." She swept her hair behind her ear and sat up some more. *Shawty feisty as hell*, I thought to myself. "You're twenty-five years old. You should have your own house for me to come see you at. I'm a grown ass woman. I shouldn't have to come over to your homeboy's crib just to see you, Thug." She finished with her mouth in a pretty pout.

"Harmony, I been hustling a long as time. It's just easier for me to move from spot to spot so the police can't keep up with a nigga. I don't have no prior employment history, but I got sixty-seven G's in cash so when I go to fill out an application to get a house and say I have all cash, but no motherfucking verification for where I accumulated it from, them motherfucking crackers gone peep that shit and next thing I know the Feds ah be at my front door. So how the fuck am I going to get a house?" The flares in her eyes softened.

"Thug, you've never worked before?"

"No."

"I had no idea you had that much got damn money. You're right. I can see how that would cause problems, but you should have gotten a job and at least kept some of it in a bank so that you could've had some way to verify some of your income. Let me do some thinking I'll find a way to help you get on your grown man shit, but in the mean time, you need to leave these thotties and these streets alone." She stood and retrieved her finger.

When she did that, all of my frustration went away. *Damn my rollie one hun'nad.* I thought to myself watching Harmony get up and walk to the bedroom door. Harmony knew how to control me in a special way without even trying. I liked the way she encouraged me to be a better nigga and shit. Maybe I did need to get a crib somewhere and get up out the hood.

"Don't go. Chill with me, bae. I'm sorry." I reached out and grabbed her arm. Harmony turned and looked in my eyes. There was something naturally magnetic between us and I knew she couldn't resist it because I couldn't resist it either. I could feel it and I knew she could too. I needed her in my world just to keep on functioning.

"No, not this time, Thug. And another damn thing, when I

leave here you need to wash your damn dick with lots of soap and scalding hot water. It's no telling where that tramp's mouth has been," she said and when she pulled away I felt my happiness leaving with her. I didn't even chase after her or get upset by what she said about Nakita's mouth.

Harmony closed the bedroom door and I walked over to the window to pull back my bedroom curtain and watched Harmony get into her car and leave. For the next few seconds, I stood all alone behind the curtain and watched her drive away. When she was completely gone, I laid on the bed staring up at the ceiling. I thought about her tears and how much I had hurt her by my actions tonight. I felt bad as hell, and right then, I realized that in order for me to be feeling some type of way about the way I treated her I must truly love bae. That's why I got up and walked towards the bathroom to shower like she commanded me to do just moments earlier. I washed my dick and I knew I was about to make some drastic changes.

CHAPTER 17
THUG

A month and a half had gone by and it had been that long since I'd heard from Harmony, no phone calls, no texts, no nothing. I had made a few changes in my life since then, not only for myself but somewhere in the back of my mind, I still wanted her. Even if I couldn't have her again, I could still make my life better for the next real woman I'd meet.

I wanted to share the good news with her, but there was no way I would call her and blab about this type of shit to someone who cut me off and stopped talking to me completely. I stopped selling weed and got a job at McDonald's. I had a few minor misdemeanors on my record, but my shit wasn't totally jacked up, so after begging the manager several times, they finally hired me. At that moment, a nigga didn't even care about putting on that corny ass uniform, I just wanted to do better and maybe one day get my ass up out the hood.

I arrived to the parking lot of McDonald's and killed the engine. It was only my third week on the job, but I was already loving not having to watch over my shoulder and shit or worry about catching a case over some bullshit.

"Terrell, as soon as you clock in, I need for you to sweep the parking lot. After that you can wash your hands and drop me some fries and by then it'll be time to relieve Tonya, so you can take her spot on the line." As soon as I walked in, I was given several instructions on what to do and when by a dark-skin chick name Kamisha. She had her hand on her hip and seemed like shawty always had an attitude. Kamisha couldn't have been no more than twenty-one, but already, she was the crew leader.

"Okay, word. I got you," I said and went to the supply room retrieved the dust pan and broom. "You want me to do the lobby, too?" I asked, because I wanted to go the extra mile, really show them how much I appreciated the job. It was way better than sitting on the block with a gun waiting for grimy niggas to pull up and buy weed, but when Kamisha turned around her demeanor went from nonchalant to irritated.

"Did I ask you to do the lobby, too? Can't you see we got customers out there, Terrell? You do have eyes, man, use them," she blurted and threw up her hands, but as she walked away I could still hear her complaining. "Damn, they just hire the dumbest motherfuckers." A few people snickered under their breaths and others just blatantly laughed out loud. I looked around at everyone who wiped the smirks from their faces and then back down at my name tag, saying Terrell Jenkins. It shimmered off the lights.

"My bad," I said and walked through the glass doors with the red and yellow McDonald's logo on it. As soon as the glass doors opened, my hands collided with a Styrofoam cup. Coffee splashed into the air and landed on my shirt and on the gentlemen in front of me.

"Crap. You clumsy asshole," a white man yelled and shoved his middle finger at me.

"I'm sorry, sir. I didn't mean to do that."

"You sure are a sorry, motherfucker," he said and brushed past me, threatening to tell my boss. I didn't even turn around to argue; I just went outside and began sweeping the parking lot, even though it took a lot out of me not to respond in my normal manner.

***

HARMONY

"Hey, Trisha, pull over there to McDonald's right quick. I

have a taste for an Oreo McFlurry," I said.

"Ooh yeah! I think I'll get me one too," she said and turned into the McDonald's parking lot and found a place to park. "Damn, the drive thru is on boom. We can just go in and get it."

I grabbed my handbag off the seat and got out of the car and looked around to wait for Trisha to join me. "Hey! Isn't that your young stud over there?" Trisha asked as we walked towards the fast food entrance.

"Where?" I said shielding my eyes from the bright beaming sunshine.

"Over there, sweeping the sidewalk," she said pointing.

By the time I saw the direction in which she was pointing, Thug just so happen to look up and caught us staring. "Go on in and make my order and get yours too," I said and reached into my handbag to retrieve my wallet. I took out a single ten-dollar bill to give to Trisha.

"Will do," she said. "Hey, Thug!" she called out before she went inside the building. Thug gave her a head nod and swept some trash into the thing he was holding.

I walked over slowly to where Thug was working. He was dressed in a McDonald's uniform and all. "Terrell Jenkins, wow!" I was surprised but found it reassuring that he kept his word to me about finding a legitimate job.

"Wats up, Miss Harmony," Thug said, but he never wavered from doing his job. I kind of missed him calling me shawty or ma but I shrugged it off. "Hey, Thug," I replied.

"I prefer you to call me Terrell while I'm working," he looked at me up and down but he never stopped sweeping the sidewalk. "I'm trying to become more of a professional after all and I gotta start somewhere," he added.

"Sure, I'm glad to see you working," I finally said after a pause.

I'm not going to lie and I'm not even going to try and kid myself, I missed my thugalicious Thug like something serious. The uniform didn't even hide his muscles or take away from his sexiness at all. I craved in that moment to do everything in my power to help him do better for himself, since he had proved to me that he wanted better for himself.

"Well, I'm sorry but I can't be seeing talking when I'm posed to be working. I see my manager glaring out the window at me," he said as he looked over my shoulder.

"I understand," I replied even though I wanted to talk to him more. "I'm going to go, but before I do, what time do you get off?" I asked him.

"Why do yo wanna kno wat time a nigga get off?" he asked reverting back to the old Thug that I knew and loved. *Omg, I just said loved, didn't I?*

"I wanted to know so you could come by my apartment later on. I could fix us dinner or I could order us something to eat." We stood there looking into each other's eyes without speaking.

"Terrell! You don't get paid to stand around yacking all day to the customers," a woman came up to us and said to Thug. She had a scowl on her face as she looked back and forth between Thug and me.

"I'm sorry, it was totally my fault," I attempted to say.

"Was I talkin' to you?" the manager who wasn't professional at all turned to me and asked.

"No but," I attempted without success to get out again.

"Terrell, if you value your job, you better get busy. I gotta mind to dock you thirty minutes for yacking anyways," she said, placing her hand on her hip.

"I'm getting back to work right now, sorry" Terrell said meekly to this thick dark chick. I'd never seen him act so civil with anyone before. I know my face had turned red because I was livid

94

on Thug's behalf for how rude this young woman was and that she held a manager's position was downright wrong on multiple levels.

I looked over at Thug and he must have been reading my mind. He gave a slight shake of his head as if to warn me not to say anything. I knew that he didn't want my words to cause him to lose his job.

"Harmony," Trisha called out to me by her car. "Are you ready to go?"

"Yeah," I said looking over my shoulder in her direction. "It was good to see you again, Terrell," I said purposely ignoring his ghetto of an ass manager, who clearly had eaten way too many Big Macs and cookies.

"Nice to see you too." He never answered me about coming over tonight for dinner or the time he would be getting off.

"I'll text you my address if you decide to come over later," I said and walked off, but Thug didn't reply.

His manager could be heard lecturing him about the rules of his job as I walked off and got in the passenger side of Trish's car.

"Why do you have that scowl on your face? It looks like you want to bitch slap somebody," she said.

"Girl, just get me away from here ASAP," I said and picked up my McFlurry that Trisha had placed in the cup holder for me.

"Ooh! You and your sexy young Thug must have had an argument."

"No, but I wanted to wrap my hands around the neck of his ghetto assed manager," I revealed. "She isn't professional at all and it burned me up inside the way she talked down to my man. He doesn't deserve that and I'm so proud of him for keeping his word about getting a legitimate job and trying to do better for himself."

"Does that mean you forgive him for letting that thot deep throat him?" she asked and glanced at me sideways as she navigated through the busy afternoon traffic.

"No, I will have that image in my head for a long time to come. I want to beat his ass even though I know I couldn't every time I think about it. Hell, I haven't even gotten a taste of the dick myself yet," I said with jealousy in my heart.

"Harmony, you put the man on a month's punishment. If you don't give that man some pussy or get you some of that fine ass dick, trust me, some of these thotties will be riding and sucking the hell out of that dick," Trisha stated.

I scowled because of her words.

"What, bitch? I broke it down and told you the simple truth. And another thing, stop acting like he's beneath you. Don't no man want to feel like a woman is better than him."

"I don't mean to act like that, I swear," I said feeling hurt by my friend's choice of words.

"I know you don't, but it comes off that way sometimes."

"Maybe I do," I said and mulled over her words in my head. "I still don't like the way that bitch treated him though. Is your job still hiring people for the mail room?" I asked her.

"Sure is," she replied and glanced at me. "Why?"

"Do you think you can get Thug hired without going through a lot of red tape, because of his record and all?"

"Actually, his record won't be a problem. We have a program on our job where we hire convicted felons and such who are trying to improve their lives. He would have to take a drug test and come in to fill out an application, but I will have my associate Lauren in human resources pull his file once he fills out the application. Do you think you can get him to come in Monday morning to get the ball rolling?" she asked.

"I will try," I replied and reached for my cell phone to type Thug a quick text with my address.

"Great! Because the mailroom starts them out at $12.50 an hour with the potential of moving up and they will pay for the employees some college courses if they desire it."

"Wow, that's a lot better than the minimum wage job he has now."

"It sure is. But he can't come up in there in Jordan's and with his pants hanging down his ass either," Trisha warned.

"I knew that already. I will be sure he's dressed appropriately, even if I have to go shopping with him," I added.

We talked some more until she pulled up to my apartment building. "Thanks for the outing and everything else," I said before getting out of her car and waving goodbye.

"Be sure to call me and let me know how tonight works out," she shouted through her open rolled down window of her car.

"I will," I assured her. I watched her pull away and walked up the stairs to my apartment. I hoped I had something to tell my friend about tonight because I wasn't even sure Thug was coming over or wanted anything else to do with me at all.

CHAPTER 18
HARMONY

I walked around my apartment and lit a couple of brown sugar candles I had bought from Bed Bath and Beyond. The aroma from the candles filled my apartment throughout with the sweet delicious smelling scent.

I wasn't sure if Thug was coming by tonight because he never responded to my text to let me know whether he was coming one way or another. The one thing that I did know was that I was going to be on my grown woman business if he did grace my apartment tonight. I wasn't going to waste another moment in getting a taste of his delectable tattooed, muscular body.

I walked back into the kitchen to check on my meal. I don't usually cook a lot unless my brother Markus comes over, but tonight I had gone all out and cooked bake chicken, homemade macaroni and cheese, collard greens, buttermilk cornbread muffins, and I had even made a sweet potato pie. If the way to a man's heart was through his stomach, then surely I was halfway there or at least I hoped that I was.

I already had taken a leisurely bubble bath and applied my favorite scents to my skin from Bath and Body Works. I had on a matching red thong bra and panty set that was trimmed in black lace under a plain, knee length, see through white shirt and nothing else. I even left my freshly pedicured feet bare. I wanted Thug to have quick access to my body because I was more than ready to devour and be devoured.

I glanced over at the clock on my wall and noted that it was a little past seven o'clock. I knew he probably had been off of work for a while. Maybe he had better plans for a Saturday night than to

98

be spending it with me. Maybe him and Nakeita had hooked up after all. I felt an overwhelming sense of jealousy run through me at the thought of him being with anybody else besides me.

"Maybe I should just forget you, Thug! Maybe I'm not the kind of woman you want in your life," I said just before I heard a knock on my door. My heart started to rapidly beat against my breastbone as I walked towards the door.

I tiptoed to look through the peephole to see who was on the other side of the door. Thug stood outside of the door with a bunch of red roses in his hand. To the backdrop of them, I could see his sexy brown eyes and the tat on his face. Thug rarely smiled, so his thug ass demeanor was such a turn on. I was so glad to see him that I smiled inwardly as I reached for the door knob and jerked the door open.

"Hey," I said becoming breathless all of a sudden from the sight of Thug. "Come on in," I beckoned him inside. Once he walked in, I closed the door behind him and ate him up with my eyes. He was dressed in all black, a pair of Gucci loafers and Gucci shirt to match, and might I add the gold chain in the center of his chest that accented his whole bad ass thuggish appearance.

"Close yo got damn mouf, man, looking all goofy and shit. You thought a nigga wasn't coming," he handed me the dozens of roses and perused me with his hazel brown eyes. My light brown nipples hardened instantly when his eyes settled on my bra covered breasts beneath the see through shirt. The thin material of the bra and shirt did nothing to hide my reaction from the heated look in his eyes.

"Shut up," I bit my bottom lip and socked him in the arm. Finally, his eyes left mine as he slowly scanned around my apartment. "Yo, dis crib nice as hell. Yo shit definitely on fleek. I cud get wit a spot like dis. Who decorated you?" he said and walked over to my living room wall to admire the artwork I had hanging on the wall.

"Yes, me, and thank you for the roses," I said feeling suddenly shy around him. It had been a month since we'd kicked it.

"Beautiful roses for a beautiful lady, but in reality da roses don't do you half justice." He licked his lips and wetness pooled between my thighs, instantaneously making me aware of him.

"Thank you," I almost stuttered. "I better put these in some water. I have a vase in the cabinet in my kitchen. You can come with me because dinner is ready," I said and walked towards the kitchen, switching my ass.

"You better cover some of that shit up. You must've known a nigga was hungry? he asked.

"I wasn't for sure, but I live in hope," I said and glanced back at him as I approached the cabinet. Thug was staring at my thonged ass through the see through shirt. I secretly smiled when I noticed the huge bulge beneath his Gucci slacks.

I turned around and opened an overhead cabinet. There was a vase on the top shelf. I inclined on my tippy toes and my shirt rose in the back. My arm was about two inches too short as I stretched to try and reach the crystal vase. "Let me help yo wit dat, ma," Thug said coming up behind me and reached for the vase with ease. "You kno yo ass too short," he said with a chuckle. He took longer than time allowed to get it, but I wasn't about to let him know that I noticed.

"Thank you," I replied and closed my eyes as he pressed closer to me, the weight of his crotch burying in between my ass. I grasped the fragile crystal vase in my hand but my mind was focused on the rigid hardness of his erection pressed against my ass cheeks.

"Mmm, you smell so good," with the vase in hand he finally bent and nuzzled my neck with a frisky rub of his nose. A slight tingle ran through me.

"We better eat!" I said suddenly as I took it from him.

What the hell is wrong with me? My pussy was pounding like my heartbeat with Thug standing this close to me. Why the hell did I have to bring up food at a moment like this, when all I really wanted to do was to have him for dinner and dessert.

"Since yo mention it, I'm ready to get my chow on. Wat kind of grub you got, ma?" he asked putting some space between us.

I hurriedly filled the vase with cold water to put the roses into before I sat them on my oval kitchen table. "Have a seat," I directed him. "I will fix both of our plates."

Thug placed his hand across his chain and seated himself at the kitchen table as I went about fixing our plates. His thick lips split into a big smile when I set his plate before him. I placed a glass of lemonade on the table for each of us as well.

"You gotta nigga feeling like a king," Thug said once I sat down at the table across from him. "Thank you, ma. I can't even remember when da last time a nigga ate a homemade meal like this," he said, staring intently across the table into my eyes.

"You're welcome. I like cooking for you," I admitted.

"Dat kind of talk touches a nigga deeply. I can see myself getting used to this type of shit," he said, dabbing his fist against his chest.

A look of surprise dawned on my face when he placed his hands on the table palms up. I quickly placed my hand in his as he blessed our food. My heart expanded even more for him as he took the initiative and time to pray over our meal.

"Juicy, you put yo foot in this shit though for real," Thug praised me. "Yo ass could open up yo own restaurant or sumthin' on da real," he said, scooping up another mouthful of macaroni and cheese onto his fork.

I glowed under his praise and took another bite myself, even though I knew that I was far from a chef, I did know my way around the kitchen. Thug was on his second piece of sweet potato pie when

I started clearing the table and putting the uneaten food in plastic containers.

"I want you to take the rest of this food with you home when you leave," I told him.

"Damn. You gone feed me and give me seconds to take home, too?" He shook his head. "Gladly!" He agreed and got up to place his plate in the sink where I was washing the dishes. He slid his arm around my waist and dumped the plate in the dishwater.

"As much food as you piled on my plate, Imma need to work dis big meal off," he said, picking up the drying cloth and dried the dishes as I washed them.

"What do you have in mind?" I asked feigning ignorance and appearing to be concentrating on rubbing the collage of soap around the glass in my hand.

"Aye, stop flexing okay. You walking around this apartment with all that ass out. You kno I wanna fuck da shit outta yo juicy ass. Which way is your bedroom?" he asked licking his lips, but I didn't answer. Thug placed the dish towel aside and turned me to face him.

He cupped my chin as I gasped from his words. With a slow prowling gaze, he slid his mouth sinuously over mine and caught my gasp inside his mouth. Forcing me to kiss him back, he slid his tongue over mine. I burned for Thug. I slipped my tongue into his mouth. His lips collided with mine once more and sought pleasure in the intimacy of the succulent kiss between us. I let the rag sink into the water and placed my arms around his neck. Thug reached down and grasped my hips and pressed towards them with a hard on. He held me so tightly that I couldn't even nudge if I wanted to.

That force that he brought along with him into my apartment was exuding lustfully. My panties became instantly soaked as I mentally prepared myself for him to make me his. I hoped I didn't have to hope for a very long time, as he dispensed all of my fears of me loving him in his thorough kiss of not only my mouth, but he kissed the deepest recesses of my soul awake.

"Do you trust me, shawty? I mean really trust me?" he asked as he muttered sexily against my kissed swollen lips.

"Yes," I whimpered my words against his delicious thick lips. I couldn't seem to get enough of his gentle, sweet kisses.

"Show me that you trust me. Show me that yo juicy ass believe in a nigga. Reassure me that you don't mind being with a nigga from the hood like me, because I wanna be that man fo you that can fulfill your every desire. I may not have always been a good nigga, but I'm willing to learn with you in my life."

I pulled reluctantly away from him and caught his larger hand in my smaller one. I brought his hand to my lips to plant a brief kiss across his knuckles. Thug blinked once and I looked at him through my desire filled eyes. "Come with me," I said and led him out of the kitchen and up the stairs to my bedroom.

Candles withered on the wall in small shadows as we entered. My bedroom was dimly lit by the set I had left on top of the end table earlier, in hopes that I would get him in my bedroom before the night was over. I let his hand go by the time we walked in my bedroom that was painted in beige and yellowish tones. I walked over to my CD player and hit the play button and R. Kelly's 12 Play slowly crooned and filled the room.

I looked over my shoulder at Thug as R. Kelly sang. He didn't see nothing wrong with a little bump and grind and neither did I for that matter. My panties became more soaked than they already were because of the lust exuding from Thug's sexy eyes.

I hoped that I didn't have too long to wait for Thug to take the initiative in taking me like I wanted him to.

"I jus want to watch you fo a minute," he finally said and kicked the bedroom door shut behind him as he walked further into the room. "It's something about me that you need to know before we take it there." he said and rubbed his lip.

"What's that?"

"If dat pussy is as good as it look, Imma want that ass all the time. I'm talking early in the morning before you go to work, on yo lunch break, and late at night, but Imma be honest with chu. I haven't fucked wit nobody else in a whole month so my nuts are fully loaded with cum. My shit throbbing rite nie as we speak so I can't promise I will be all gentle and shit. Can yo ass handle dat?"

I backed away from him as he walked toward me. A feral look had entered his eyes.

"Take off yo clothes," he demanded in a gruff voice laced with sexual need.

Although the look in his eyes frightened me some, it also excited me too. Our eyes never wavered from each other as we took off our clothes. The music filled the room, adding to the sexual energy circulating between us and I found myself imagining us in several positions. Those presumptive images faded as he finally took off his boxers and I saw that dick. It was pointed in my direction and it was super long. *Got damn, Thugalicious.* I thought about it and wondered if I could take it all.

We both stood naked and bare. I backed up to the bed until the back of my knees touched it. "Please," I said as he stalked toward me with a ten-inch erection standing at full attention.

"Easy, shawty," he said when he came face to face with me.

The delicious virile smell of his cologne hit my nostrils and sent my sexual awareness of him into a twister of a tailspin. My need for him had my whole body trembling with my need for him.

"Imma make love to you, but Imma get nasty wit it," Thug stated with such confidence that my passion began to leak from my pussy down the inside of my thighs.

When Thug talked nasty like that, he sent a mental image spiraling out of control straight through my mind. I could see our bodies slapping together in unison as he whispered sweet words of romance and love to me. He told me I was his woman while I gasped, "You're my man," while he pumped into me again and again, easily all night long. All I wanted or needed was to be in his arms replaying round one over adding new positions into round two. This time, I was the aggressor giving it to him too. He would whisper sexily and lick his thick fuckalicious lips.

"Take that and that and that times twelve, like twelve play," he said. "While I ride you not to hell, but to somewhere that's pleasurable beyond our imaginations."

Then I said, "When you have me cumming, soaking up your shaft as well as the sheets and I'm calling you daddy or whatever else comes to mind and you get behind and take your time as we combine our juices…easy like a most fuckalicious night. Nothing like making love to you my love all night long, curled up on the bed, thinking of the many scrumptious things we could be doing together."

Like him whispering into my ear, soon followed by his snake like tongue, and then a nibble to my lobe. He gave me the chills as he pulled my shirt slightly off one shoulder, and bit gently like a vampire's kiss. I trembled ever so slightly as he gazed into my eyes and he received me as his own. I saw my reflection in his hazel eyes, and he saw his reflection in my blue ones.

Then he said, "Get on your hands and knees right now, Harmony! I want yo ass too bad for foreplay. I'll give yo ass foreplay later, much later."

CHAPTER 19
THUG

"Shid, ma, you keep looking at me like that, yo ass gon' have me cumming all over your tits and shit," I shed my pants and climbed on top of Harmony and shoved my dick in between her tits. I wanted her sexy ass from the day we met. I never told her this, but I was addicted to me some redbone and watching her, watch me fuck her tits had me wanting this grown woman in my life forever.

I rammed my dick in between her tits, I made love to them. I titty fucked her laying heavy pipe in between those soft round curves. "You a hoe. You a freaky ass hoe." I called her names as a rubbed her nipples as I drug my dick and balls across her chest, stopping right at her mouth. The more my dick rammed against her tits and chin, the closer I was getting to a super explosion.

"Oh my goodness, you're such a freak, Thug." She said in a low tone that made me fall deeper for her. I liked the way she talked, walked, and treated me. I ain't never had a real woman before and to be on top of one with my dick and balls on her chest just made me shoot my load all over her body.

"Ah fuck!" the first creamy thick load splashed all over her chin and mouth. As it dissolved, I rubbed it in with the tip of my dick head. I was hoping she liked that type of shit and I needed her to let me have my way because I was just getting started.

I kissed her softly on the side of her neck, ribs, and thighs. When I was through seeing her squirm, I sucked her pretty ass toes. I went back up to her pelvic area and kissed it while I finger fucked her. Harmony opened her legs and let me do it. As I gave her my tongue and finger work she moaned for more. She raked her nails over the silk sheets.

"Ah, fuck! I'm cuming," she yelled and spread her legs further apart. A large splash of wetness hit me in the face as she squirted. I rubbed it in my face and licked my fingers.

"Put your head right here." I stood and ushered her head to the edge of the bed. Her hair flung towards the floor as she kept her head in position. I cupped her chin and slid my nutty glazed dick back into her mouth and started fucking it.

I humped her mouth like we were fucking in circular motions. Harmony reached her hand around my ass and guided me into her face for more, by then I knew she liked to have her mouth fucked. "Juh like dat, you pretty little slut," I said as I felt her other hand snatch my shaft and started stroking it hard. I couldn't even lie to myself no more, "I love you," I blurted feeling the pressure of her squeeze. Harmony wouldn't let it go. She kept jerking it into her face and watched for the second nut. Just seeing that sexy glimmer in her eyes of wanting it so badly, had me on edge. "You bitch you!" I skeeted all in her mouth.

"Thug, please fuck me, baby. Fuck me now." Harmony wiped her mouth and leaped onto the bed. She was on all fours and looked over her shoulder at me.

"Nah, I don't want it. You not horny enough yet." I shook my head and reached for my clothes when stopped me and grabbed on the arm.

"Thug, come on, I do want it. Please don't leave me hanging," she begged. I tossed my clothes.

"Lay yo ass on yo stomach," I demanded and walked over to the candle. I took it off the stand and walked back over to the bed to find Harmony face down obediently. I climbed in the bed with the candle in my hand. "You said you can take it, right?"

"Yes," she whispered with her eyes still closed. I hovered the heated candle over her back, watching the flame flicker and let the first drop of burning wax fall.

"Ouch!" She squirmed at the sensation. I lowered my tongue and licked the spot and soothed her pain. "What the hell are you doing back there? That shit hurts." When she tried to look back, I forced another drop upon her. "Ooh," she moaned and groaned.

I crawled up to her head and lowered the blaze behind her neck. The small blaze of fire withered away from her skin trying to get back to the candle, but I repositioned it until I was sure it would burn.

"Oh my god, mmmmm," she moaned for my erotic behavior. I leaned down and sucked the back of her neck and she began squirming uncontrollably. I dropped a few more drops of hot wax down the center of her back and got up. I walked over to the table and placed it back.

"Thug, I want you," she sat up, so I laid on my back and let her have the dick. When she climbed on top of me, I felt her pussy spread around my dick. I could tell Byron hadn't been hitting it right. It was snug and juicy. I had a little trouble getting to the back, but when I worked my way through her grooves, I was in her G-spot. "Right there," she rode that dick like a pro.

I had been waiting on this moment since the day I met her pretty ass. *Got damn teacher on my dick!* I thought watching Ms. Harmony Fletcher make the sexiest fuck faces I had ever seen. If this is what being with a real woman was like, then I sure as hell wanted it. I would boss up and be that real man of her dreams. I could keep that job and work my way up, leave Gator and nem alone and them streets too. I thought about how much I was falling for her and if I should give her the gift I had in my pants pocket tonight. I had gotten an extra key made to my apartment and I wanted her to have it. I didn't know, but it's something about this grown ass woman that got me so got damn addicted to her. All I knew is whenever she's around, I fell deeper for her love.

CHAPTER 20
THUG

Gator got out. He'd called my phone a few times, but I didn't answer. I would just chop it up with him face to face. I must've checked my phone a dozen times just to see if Harmony had called or texted when I was at work. Days had gone by and her pussy was stained on me. Not only was she constantly on a nigga mind, but I found myself thinking about her every time I heard certain songs. That grown ass pussy had my nose wide the fuck open. That's why as soon as I got off today, I was going to deposit my first paycheck in the bank and stop by Gator's to tell him I was gone lay low on selling weed for a while.

A nigga couldn't believe the next day after I left my shawty's crib, I got a call from Trisha giving me the address at some microbiology lab where she's a top notch microbiologist over there. She told a nigga to come dressed his finest with none of that baggy ass shit wit the pants hangin' showin' off ass crack or underwear. Trisha broke it down for a nigga. Unlike Harmony, that Trisha got sum undercover ghetto in her ass, but that's aight too, shawty cool with me.

I went in dat Monday morning, dressed in a white shirt and black slacks. I had on some black leather loafers on my feet. Deep down, I knew dat Harmony was the one that initiated her friend to call me bout the job in the mail room. All I had to say was if I got the job, it would be a hella betta than werkin at McDonalds wit that mean ass Kamisha breathing down my neck. I swear that chick sweated me from the first day I was hired.

Anyway, I got the job in the mailroom on the same day I filled out the application. The only thing was, I had to come in the next day to do a piss test to make sure I wasn't doing drugs and shit. You know I had an answer for dat too. Suffice it to say, I passed the test and I've been werkin in the busy mailroom ever since. A nigga was as legitimate as he cud git, so that's why I drove through traffic and pulled into the nearest Regions bank. I needed to get myself solidified and this was gon' be da first step.

"May I help who's next?" There was a white lady sitting behind the counter wearing a grey top.

"Yes, ma'am, I'd like to open up a savings account, please," I said. She handed me a clipboard with a stack of papers attached and pointed me in the direction of a set of cubicles.

"New accounts are generally handled by our savings specialist. You'll need to fill out these forms and give the to the lady name Laura Flemings." I took the clipboard from her.

"Thanks." I walked over and filled out the papers. It felt good as hell to be on a better path and shit, I couldn't even lie. With the new job opening coming up that Harmony had mentioned, who knows how far a nigga could go. I was actually thinking that meeting Harmony was a good thing.

It only took me about twenty minutes to open the account and when the lady asked how much I was depositing, I told her the whole thang.

***

I pulled up to Gator's and got out, but the gaze I was met with was completely different from the one I had expected. "Bruh, tell me you not fucking with Harmony Fletcher."

Gator had called me from Bree's phone and said he had gotten out of jail. He had also mentioned that she had told him I held her down and then left her hanging too, so I could feel him on that part, but why the fuck was he eyeballing me about my woman?

"Yea, nigga, I fucks with shawty the long way. What's it to you?"

"Nigga, I'm fucking her too," he said.

Before I knew it, I snapped. I leaped from where I was standing and started choking Gator the fuck out. "Nigga, that's my girl. She ain't fucking your fat, dirty ass nigga." The more I squeezed, the more his eyes rolled to the back of his head. Bree ran outside and jumped on my back.

"Let my brother go, nigga," she yelled and I slung her like a ragdoll. Just as she hit the ground, two police cars pulled up. "The police coming!" Bree continued to scream, but I was too far gone, mad crazy with brutal anger and resentment when Gator said some fucked up shit about fucking wit my Harmony. The same Harmony that harmonized my soul and made me want to be a betta nigga.

Gator and I rolled and tussled on the ground until I finally had the upper hand and landed on top. My right hand landed in a one two three upper cut on his left jaw. He tried his best to get in a couple of good punches but I didn't even feel the pain cause the pain was too great in my heart and left me numb to anything else. By da time I got my last good punch in, I felt a pair of hands on my neck pulling me off of Gator.

Both of us were cussing and still tryna git at each other. Bree was crying and shit talkin' junk bout us fighting ova an old ass sadity bitch. You kno dis was down da po-po alley to be driving up in da hood to find nigga's fighting and shit. There goes my job and new start all cause of Gator and the woman that made me let my guard down and fall in love.

"Alright, now break it up and stop struggling or circumstances will get real ugly really quick. Jamison, take that one over there," he said pointing to Gator who was tryna get loose to get at me again. "Byron Martin, if I were you I'd settle down."

"Shid, let em go," I shouted. "If he feenin' fo sum mo of dis ass kickin' let em bring it," I said breathing hard readying myself to kill his ass with my bare hands.

111

"Shut up or I'm going to have to carry you both into lock up and we really don't want to do that if we don't have to. Are you hurt, Miss?" said the red faced officer whose name tag read Lazenby, he directed his words to Bree.

I clamped my mouth shut and tried to bring my anger under control as I looked over at Bree, who was like a lil sister to me. I didn't mean to scare her but shit had got real when Gator said dat fucked up shit.

"I'm alright," Bree finally said once she got her crying under control. "I just want dem to stop fightin'. I don't want dem to go to jail," she sobbed sum mo.

"Nobody's going to jail, young lady," said the officer as he checked me for weapons.

"This one has no weapons on him," called out the other officer. "It looks like it they had a misunderstanding of some sort. Since no property was damaged, or no deadly weapons to be found, I say we let them off with a warning this time, but if we have to come on this side of town for the same thing next time they both go to jail."

"I agree," said Lazenby. "Which one of you live here?" asked Lazenby.

"Dis my crib," answered Gator.

"Well, sir, I suggest you get in your car and leave right now," said Lazenby giving me a stern look.

I looked over at Gator and threw him a threatening glance. This was far from over, my glance alerted him. He put his finger to his head like a gun and pulled the trigger when the cops weren't looking. That was a threat and I didn't take threats likely. There was nothing I could do if I didn't want to carry my ass to jail. So I left with the police car riding behind me until I took a right turn about five miles down the highway at the traffic light. In fifteen minutes or so, I would be at Harmony's apartment and shit wasn't gon' be pretty! You can fuckin' believe dat.

CHAPTER 21
HARMONY

Thug had been on my mind a lot ever since the night he rocked my world. Nobody had ever touched my heart or soul in the way he had, not even Byron with his lying ass, who never let me come to his apartment or introduced me to his family. I had even introduced him to my brother Markus because I thought we had something serious going on until the day I caught him in my apartment screwing that whore. I would never forgive his ass for hurting me in the way he did.

But today was a new day and I had Thug in my life and it was time for me to bring the two men that meant the most to me together. I couldn't avoid it any longer; I knew that I needed to set up a meeting between him and Markus very soon. Thug had proven to me he could be the man I needed, trusted and wanted in my life. Now it was time for me to prove that I could be the woman for him. I loved him just that much, so much that I even surprised myself.

I had been avoiding the chance for Thug and Markus to meet, even though Trisha had gotten Thug a job in the mailroom at her job and he no longer had to work at McDonald's. I knew that Markus would still feel some type of way about me dating Thug's type.

I was a grown ass woman though. He didn't have to like my decision to date Thug. He just had to respect me enough as his baby sister to live my life and be happy on my own terms and not by his own high expectations of what my life should be like. That's why I planned on inviting Thug and my brother over to my apartment to have them in the same place under my roof to introduce them. I just prayed and hoped they got along.

Bam, Bam, Bam! I was snatched from my musings as I flipped through the television with the remote control I had in my hand. "Open the got damn door, Harmony!" I could hear Thug's angry voice on the outside of my apartment door, shouting.

I jumped up off of the couch and ran to the door thinking that someone was after him or he could be hurt. The first thing I noticed was the blood on the side of his mouth and shirt. "What's wrong?" I gasped, after opening the door but fell back as I saw the vexed look radiating from Thug's eyes and it was directed at me.

"Why da hell didn't yo slut ass tell me dat you fucking my nigga?" he said slamming the door so hard behind him that it rattled against its hinges.

"I don't know what you're talking about. I promise you I'm not sleeping with anybody but you," I said shocked by the absurdity of his accusations. "How can you call me a slut, after what we just shared? I love you and only you," I promised him as I reached out to him but he slapped my hands away.

"Don't yo slimy ass dare touch me or I swear I'll choke yo bitch ass to death with my bare hands," he threatened as he clenched and unclenched his hands at his sides.

"Why are you treating me this way?" Tears brimmed in my eyes and fell down my cheeks. I took the back of my hand to wipe the tears away but more tears fell in their place.

"Look me in my damn eyes and tell me yo ass ain't fucking my nigga, Gator," he said as he stepped to me, looking down on me like if I didn't answer in the right way that my life might be in danger.

"I'm not fucking your nigga, Gator. I promise you," I said looking up into his stormy hazel eyes. "I swear on my parent's graves that I don't even know a Gator. Wherever your information is coming from you are being misinformed."

"Let me be clear, if yo ass fucking lying to me, Juicy, there will be consequences," he said before a knock at the door interrupted us.

My eyes and Thug's collided. I wasn't expecting company and I hoped that my brother hadn't showed up unannounced. I didn't want them to meet under these circumstances.

The knock at the door intensified. "Open the door, Harmony," Thug demanded.

"Okay," I said softly and walked slowly to the door. I took a deep breath and wiped away my tears away before I opened the door.

"Baby," Byron stepped through the door all bloody as if he had just been in an altercation of some sort.

What the hell was Bryon doing showing up at my apartment? I hadn't seen him since the day I first met Thug and he was waiting for me on my apartment doorstep. I could feel the hairs on the back of my neck standing up as if electrically charged. I turned around as if in slow motion to see the irate expression on Thug's face.

"Baby! Why dis nigga, Gator, callin' yo ass 'baby?" Thug asked me with a look of betrayal on his handsome face, which was twisted up with outrage at the moment.

"What da hell yo ass doing in my woman's house, nigga?" asked Bryon. Byron was the only name that I knew him by.

"I...I," I tried to say as my heart lurched and my breath caught in my throat. The crazy world as I knew it had begun to spiral out of control as the man that I loved stood over me with a look of hurt and disdain radiating from his eyes.

The words I tried to say were lodged deep in my throat as I tried to force them up and past my shocked and confused mind. No words would force past my frozen lips. I was frozen without the ability to comply with the synchronicity of my brain.

"So you sayin' you don't know this nigga?"

"Yeah, I know him, but not as Gator!" The words finally slipped past my lips. "I know him as…"

"Fuck you, bitch. I don't need dis shit. Fuck this, I'm outta here," Thug suddenly said before walking angrily towards the door and opening it. "Yawls two lame asses can have each other," he said and walked out.

"Thug!" I finally found my voice as big fat tears fell from my eyes. I attempted to run towards the door to stop him from leaving me, but Bryon a.k.a. Gator, swept me up around my waist to keep me from going after my thugalicious Thug. The one that changed me from the moment he had entered my world. Without him, I knew nothing would never ever be the same again.

THE END

To every reader that purchase our book, we humbly thank you. We hope you enjoy our first collaboration together. We truly enjoyed writing it. Until next time...

Best wishes, always,
RESA & JROC

THUGS AND ROSES

A Brick City Projects Love Story

by JRoc

CHAPTER 1
THE INTRO TO THIS SHIT
Thugs & Roses of Brick City Projects

A windy, almost grungy and daunting current misted through the air one Saturday afternoon, right after a light storm had subdued. The sky looked dismal and gloomy. A limited drizzle flickered from the sky, falling unto rusted sewer tops and a car drove by splashing the residue of rain on both sides of the tire. It was those comforting sounds of restoration you'd hear just after a storm had backed off and made the skies calm again. The eerie atmosphere settled in a smokeless, murky haze. It was nothing short of the devil's playground; Cincinnati, Ohio, also known as Nati, to be exact. The land where the curbs reeked of America's most notorious, black hooded muggers, sleazy purse snatchers, and cold-blooded killers. It was one of those days when you could just feel that something was brewing in the air.

The prowling feet of a few junkies and some grimy niggas stood anxiously on the side of the street in the section they called The Tops of Brick City Projects. The large concrete cage held the type of niggas that would run up on you and put that burner in ya' face at any given unexpected moment. The rest of the Nati drove by fearing the nappy dread heads they'd seen roaming about inside this cage.

Society was horrified by the illusion that "the animal" was on the loose, if approached by one of these nappy-headed thugs out in the public. People wouldn't look them in the eye and some even rolled up their windows when they saw them coming. They were all here, compacted inside of this gated housing project called Brick City.

Most hadn't come back outside after the rain yet, but there were a few who were already standing on scales of trouble.

"Aye Bunz, there go that nigga Freddy!" a fiending bystander snitched, with the crummy odor of putrid bile fuming from his lips. His breath was funkier than a muthafuckin' sports shoe. The crud around his mouth looked like he'd been eating a pound of white powdered donuts, but everyone knew that wasn't the case.

Throwing a few street-coded hand signals and an odd facial gesture that made him look even uglier, the fiend sauntered from one side of the street, while scratching his nuts. Before he'd known it, he stepped in a pot hole full of rain water fencing his dirty feet with a much needed wash up. His Crocs and toes were soaking wet, but he didn't stop right then; he stumbled to the other side and onto the curb in no time.

"Got damn! Fucking up my good shoes and shit! I spent a hun'nad and twenty seven zillion dollas on these Air Jordan's. I oughta come back there and back slap yo' ass!" The fiend had looked back at the puddle and rambled a bunch of nonsense afterwards. Nigga didn't even have on no Jordan's.

He was as black a slave fresh off the boat from the motherland like in the movie *Roots* and as fidgety as Pookie in *New Jack City*. Wearing a torn white tee-that showcased a dingy-ass collar, his neckline lay lower than usual from being stretched unreasonably during times when he'd been in need of a fix and had pulled on it inconsiderately and from far too many days of being rubbed against the filthy alley brick walls where he'd kneeled down to hit the crack pipe or suck a few dicks. This stanking-ass nigga was just another fiend hoping to gain some brownie points with Bunz, who ran the Top part of Brick City projects right off St. Bernard. Though it was hella G's moving through the concrete cage, Bunz was the one with the most work up Top.

Bald-headed and weighing two hundred and twenty five pounds, Bunz shoulda been out of the game a long time ago, but he was one of those ole school cats that was never gon' leave the hood. He had a thick-ass roll on the back of his head that looked like a hot dog, the kind you'd want to just walk up on and chop off, shit's ridiculous. Every time he turned around, you'd see it.

The fiend was trying to remain discreet while buttering up the info, giving Bunz a heads up on Freddy, who owed Bunz five bucks after being short when he copped from him two days ago. Freddy had been dodging Bunz.

When you owed money in the hood, everybody knew. Once a nigga didn't see yo' ass on the scene like you'd usually be, it made you look suspect so word would whisper, "Anybody seen Freddy ole scheming ass lately?"

Freddy knew Bunz's spot was The Tops. He knew Bunz would be posted up right off St. Bernard working the corners as usual, but apparently crackheads think it slips dealers' minds or something 'cuz they always try that slick shit.

After seeing Freddy's slumped shoulders hiding behind the blue car that had just pulled up across the street, Bunz reached into his baggy jeans and pulled out the black nine millimeter. It was slightly weathered with silver scuff marks on the side and old scratches around the handle from previous pistol whippings and gunplay. It was worn, but it could still be used to fire ah nigga's ass up real quick.

Just a few feet away from it all was Freddy's nephew, a scrawny peon named Lil Rich. He was a puny little nigga that walked like he didn't belong around the way. His goofy-ass walk signaled the word "square" coming down the block. He had long, skinny legs that barely even bent when he walked. Wearing a random pair of khakis, a multicolored vestie, and some dusty-ass Converse, he gave the word cornball true meaning. On the real, this squirt looked like Goofy the cartoon character as he took a stroll. He had a chipped tooth in the front of his mouth, a mini Afro, and ah American bandanna folded around his head, which was the only feature that even made him fit into the whole array of things.

Though Lil Rich was only twelve, he seemed to have his head on pretty straight. Lil Rich didn't bother nobody and most kept their jokes to a muffled chatter, but nobody really fucked with him. He could've fixed that bandana though, tucked it a little better, just enough to accent his lame-ass features, because it was currently crooked, showing the uncombed wads of his nappy ass hair. It made him look slouchy as fuck and not to mention very young-minded.

Freddy had just left the crib moments ago, leaving Lil Rich all alone and all the food was gone. Lil Rich had checked the refrigerator as soon as his uncle had left but only found empty disappointment. He was on his way to the corner store, which was just up the block. Coming from up Top where he stayed, Lil Rich would have to cross the Bottoms to get there, which was territory of their rivals. Them Bottom niggas. The ones they always had beef with. That's where Psycho Ced and them stayed. But first Lil Rich had to make it from the Tops because it was a war zone as well.

The clanking sound of dimes and quarters that whirled around in his pocket played a soft verse of *I'm poor as hell* as he strolled looking down at the random lines in the sidewalk. He had scrounged up some change to get a single pack of Ramen noodle and a Faygo pop. Arabs broke them shits down into single packs for the hood.

Lil Rich had almost made it to the end of the street but action like this was too hard to ignore.

"Aye, bitch! Where m-m, mmmmmy five dah-dah dollars at?"

Bunz had a bad-ass stuttering problem, but there wasn't a muthafucka on this side of the Nati that was brave enough to test Bunz's gangsta, nobody except for crazy ass Psycho Ced, but he was posted in the Bottoms of Brick City and since the niggas at the Tops didn't fuck with the niggas at the Bottom, they had no reason to even cross paths.

Up Top, everybody knew not to test Bunz on no humbug shit. They knew what Bunz ah do to that ass. After he beat down two other muthafuckas with a crowbar and shot a few, they stayed out of his way and he stayed to himself. Niggas had their own li'l duck-offs in his section.

At age forty-one, Bunz was still working the corner. He was too stingy to pay anyone to work the block for him, and he'd already seen too many niggas pull that sucker shit on the hands that fed them, so his trust issues were fucked up.

Bunz wanted to see every dollar that came in. He had a real fetish for counting it and holding it in his hands, flipping it over, that type of shit. Bunz liked to lay his paper in piles of fives, twenties, and hun'nads, then smoke a blunt while recounting it again. I guess it made him feel powerful. So with that being said, he needed that five that Freddy owed him.

Freddy tried to hide behind an old-ass Honda Civic that was cruising by slowly, looking for dope. It was always some white muthafucka riding through asking, "Who got the butter?"

Bunz would handle the cluck in a minute. Right now, he had tunnel vision on Freddy's ass.

"I see y-y-y-y-yo' s-s-s-sced ass, nigga!" Bunz walked faster, pulling up his britches that were sagging like them young cats, trying his best to catch Freddy slipping.

The nine, call that bitch "Nina," was pointing at the moving car. Bunz knew Freddy was on the other side of it and, at the moment, he didn't give a fuck who got blasted.

Even at his age, he was trying to keep his swag on at least medium, though he wasn't really that coordinated wearing that black Cincinnati Bengals jersey and those denim Rocawear jeans.

He made a quick dash, revving up his curled-up wheat Timbs to catch Freddy, gun still pointed hastily in that direction with his finger on the trigger. He used his other arm to embrace the BUNZ charm that was dangling on his neck.

He finally caught up to the car with a mean-ass glare sketched across his face, eyes inflamed with dark flares of violence below the wrinkles of his forehead. Without hesitating, his index finger began pulling the trigger. These circumstances and temperaments were why innocent people ended up on the news, 'cuz the impatient Bunz snapped.

CHAPTER 2
THE BOTTOMS

"Yo Money, whip that soda extra thin. One of these birds flying tomorrow. I gotta make this shit come back like pussy, nigga." There was no chance at hiding his twelve golds when he said that shit. Though it was a bunch of shooters prowling the hood, Psycho Ced was the most ruthless nigga in the Bottoms of Brick City at the time.

Much associated with his name, everybody called him Psycho. He was six foot three inches of pure muscle. Having shortly gotten out of prison, he still paraded a uncultured, monstrous attitude. His demeanor was aggressive and intimidating to others. He was dark-skinned, crude, and uncivilized. America's worst nightmare. His words were always intrusive and hostile, spooking any soft nigga away from his presence. Psycho hated pussy-ass niggas.

Broad at the shoulders with too many fucking tats to name, Psycho was a walking beast. But on this day in particular, he was inside the trap spot hovered over two birds of pure cocaine, enough to send all them niggas to the pen for a while; him, Money, and the rest.

Most were wearing baggy jeans with a hoody covering the tops of their foreheads. Underneath were partially shaded, black, and forgotten faces. There were no laughs, no smiles…only solid stonework from the hands of poverty, and a hustling spirit to get it by any means necessary.

Their pain was unspoken, hidden behind that deep and distant look. It wasn't hard to see that cold and icy glare of oppression that grazed them deeply behind the blinking of their eyes, just black; unfriendly faces that were void, troubled, and empty. As far as they were concerned, minimum wage was bullshit, so they came together to form a click…a click of thugs.

There were twelve in all seated at the round table: shooters, robbers, thugs, and hustlers, all devoted to the cause. Each of them was crafty at his own larrikin skill and Psycho knew just how to pawn them like a game of chess.

Most of them were sitting reservedly with their arms folded as they watched him. As head of the crew, he kept his Glock 40 where mu'fuckas could always see it, right on his dick. No one really knew when Psycho was gone snap or pop off. It was just one of those things you'd have to hang around him to sorda know and even then…you still didn't know. He was a strapped bomb slowly ticking, just waiting to go off at any given moment.

Though he'd only been home three years from doing a bid, he'd ranked back to position in no time with the help of Money. Though before he'd only run a smaller crew of five, Psycho was ready.

Psycho grew up in Dayton watching his father, Poochie, sell weed out of their garage, so he was familiar with the way things ran. Never get too flashy, always stay strapped and never trust no one. He was sitting outside on the hood of the car one day when some niggas pulled up, asked for his dad and then capped his ass in broad daylight. Psycho remembered those days of trapping with crystal clarity.

His father was a good dude 'til he got killed by some of his own. Big Mike, who used to run Dayton, had paid some homies of Poochie's to murk him because he wanted Poochie's pussy (Ced's mom) and his trap spot.

Yeah, Psycho Ced remembered just how shady the game could be, and he would make sure no nigga on his team would try that slick shit. He would end up trapping too, just like his ole dude, but the only problem was that Psycho was a hot head and niggas like him didn't take no mu'fuckan orders from nobody. He didn't want nobody bossing him; that's why he ran his own shit.

Branded by haunted memories, his knuckles pressed firmly into the round table made of oak. His long-ass dreads slung to the front, hanging like a bunch of black ropes, leaving behind a shaded sketch of corruption. In between, his twenty-four inch platinum chain displayed a twinkled bling of the Lord's supper. His charm was for sporty purposes, nothing more. After seeing so many of his homies get shot and killed, Psycho didn't believe in no God, point blank period. Below the necklace sat a chiseled tray of thug'ish abs. Most of them were marked with random street names and gang insignia tattoos. Even though he'd murked four out of the nine niggas he'd shot, they were still remembered. He had a couple of war wounds to prove it.

Money was rapping to himself and more cocaine was pushed into the bag. Psycho watched the hands of his goon with grim eyes. Money, being a vet to the game of hustle'nomics, dropped the Pyrex onto the table and threw an ounce on the scale weighing exactly 28.3 grams. He always got that shit perfect.

"Bruh, I told you shit was gone start jumping off for us. See when you got the right product, niggas gone shop with you. Don't even trip, I got you. We already got shit sewed up. Niggas can't get even a got-damn two piece from Popeye's, since we hit 'em off with the new work. Them niggas is broke son," Money announced looking up at his compadre. "Who getting a bird though?"

Ced took a seat.

"Lucky-ass nigga yo! How the fuck you do that shit?" He glorified the sleekness of Money's trap skills and then sat back in the wooden chair with his two hands together in an upright praying position watching, his eyes calculating Money's every move with a slippery glare.

Money smirked an ace face. Money was a clean-cut nigga who always kept a crispy-ass edge up. Nigga looking like Omar Epps and shit, except his face was more scrubby, more hood. Ced let Money handle the scales 'cuz Money was good at math. Shid, Money was the reason Ced had gotten up to five birds. Every boss nigga needed a nigga like Money on the team. That's how he got the name Money, from Psycho.

Dark-skinned looking like cheddar, Money was one of those smart and skillful dudes. Having graduated from Akin High as valedictorian showed his accumulated knowledge in more ways than one. Money was no joke when it came to numbers and being a king to the wise if it ever came time to checkmate. Money knew how to be intelligent and grimy at the same time and Psycho knew that.

"This li'l hook up I used to slang to back in the day. I bumped into him the other day, told him we got some work and he hit me up. I may need you to take it for me though; I got something lined up for later on tonight," Psycho said.

"Oh, word that. Aye, if you take a li'l of dat shake off each bag and pile it in another zip, we'll have some extra grams of free work. Give it to these niggas, let them sample it! You said you wanted to make shit jump back, right?" Money nonchalantly summoned the proposal in a cool way to let Psycho feel like it was totally his idea. Money was a fucking genius.

"Yeah, I was thinking the same thing!" Psycho ensconced a slight smirk, hiding it behind his sleek mask.

"True, true," said Money, weighing it up and bagging more work into the clear Ziploc.

"Say, Money," he took a drag from the Newport he'd just lit, coughed two times then blew out the remainder of smoke through his flaring nostrils. "You ever thought you'd be getting paper like dis nugga?" Psycho asked. Even though he was a snake, he still created small talk. He knew that as long as they were getting money, he was getting money.

Psycho knew how to talk to niggas and get them to do anything he said. It was his way of kinda patting his niggas on the back, but also making sure they wanted to keep doing dirty work with him. That way, he'd know if he needed to off one of them niggas with the burner. He was just that raw, real greasy with the mouf play.

"This little bread to me nigga. I mean, I can lace shorty up, stay fly and pay a few bills, but you know me. I like them super bands though. I wasn't born to be rocking no li'l-ass scooter across town. Nigga, I needs me one of those big boys like a G Class Benz! I know I can't get that shit working at no fuckin' McDonald's. I just didn't think I'd end up selling dope."

Money was cool. He knew not to let Psycho get in his head all the time. He let Psycho know he had sense, unlike them other niggas on the team.

Money wasn't totally relying on Psycho. He would get his financial aid, then flipped it, buy his own pack and grind on the side. This also allowed him time away from the heat in the infamous trap spot at the Bottoms. They pumped out of a two bedroom apartment that was leased to Money's baby momma, Tameka. She was on section 8. Money needed an alibi, so he chose part-time courses at U.C. 'cuz living this life day in and day out could catch up with you when you least expected it and today would be one of those days he'd wished he took his ass to class.

YOU'RE THE ONE FOR ME
by Theresa Hodge (aka Resa)

PROLOGUE
May 15, 1999

Damon

I sprayed a generous amount of Burberry cologne into the air and walked through the mist. I had a fresh cut and had on my freshest clothes. I was on my way out to pick Anne-Marie up for our senior dance. I couldn't wait to see her pretty face. I started putting on my shoes superfast as I thought about how sexy she would look when I picked her up. I loved Anne-Marie with all my heart. In fact, my heart was beating to the syllables of her name.

I had every intention to make her my wife once I finished college and got a job where I could take care of her. I wanted to give her everything a real man gives to his woman. We both would be graduating next week and I couldn't wait for the day to come that we could be together all the time.

"Come in here, son," dad said as I was finishing up getting dressed. "Your mom and I want to talk to you for a minute," he added with a stern voice.

I wondered what I had done wrong. I hoped like hell I wasn't in trouble. I wouldn't know how to act if they told me I couldn't go to this dance.

I walked into the living room and found my mother and father sitting down as if they were preparing for a church board meeting. My mother had a look of distress on her face. She wouldn't even look at me.

"Damon," mom said rising from her seat. She went to

stand beside my father, the great Pastor Damon Williams Sr.

I figured she was using my father as a crutch to give her strength to say whatever it was she wanted to say to me.

"We need to talk to you before you go out tonight," she added.

"What's this about?" I asked stepping fully into the room.

"Have a seat, son," dad said pointing to a chair across from the sofa.

I sat down and waited for my parents to take their seats on the sofa. I glanced at my watch impatiently. I didn't want Anne-Marie to have to wait. I knew how impatient she could get at times. I wished they would get on with whatever they wanted to talk about.

Dad looked me in my eyes and cleared his throat before he began speaking. "Son, you are young and you have your whole life in front of you. Your mom and I," he said looking over at my mom. "We have been talking and we decided that you shouldn't see that Johnston girl anymore."

I looked at them as if they had lost their natural minds. "Why do you think that?" I asked with a frown.

"Well for one thing, she's fast in the tail. She doesn't carry herself like a young lady should. She comes around here flouncing around in those itty bitty shorts," said mom with disdain covering every word. "She has no respect whatsoever for the pastor and I. Isn't that right, honey?" she huffed as she asked my father to corroborate her opinion.

Dad looked over at me uncomfortably. He knew how much I loved Anne-Marie. I'd told him when we had one of our many man-to-man talks.

"That's right sweetheart," he agreed with mom. "She just doesn't carry herself befitting of a young Christian lady with good values, son. She comes from a single mother who works all the time just to keep a roof over their heads. She's practically raising herself and we want you to have someone better than that in your life."

"That's right," mom picked up where dad left off.

"But the fact that she doesn't have a father in her house, and her mother is struggling to pay their bills, is all the more reason we should accept her into our family," I reasoned.

I couldn't understand for the life of me why my father would get up in that pulpit and preach about what Jesus would do and what we as Christians should do and then turn his back on someone who needed him to uplift them.

They looked at each other. Dad began to speak but mom shook her head.

"Son, my only responsibility is you," she said. "And you'll be going away to college in the next couple of months. You don't need the excess baggage holding you back." Mom looked like she wanted to say trash instead of baggage, but one could always count on her to be politically correct.

"Well, I love Anne-Marie and I ain't breaking up with her!" I said angrily. I didn't understand why mom never liked Anne-Marie, when she went out of her way to treat her respectfully.

"Now, you know I don't play that raising your voice in this house. You will respect your mother and me. I don't care how old you get," dad said in a voice that brooked no argument.

I bit back my reply. I stared angrily at my parents as they teamed up against me and the love of my life. "I'm sorry," I mumbled without looking either of them in the eyes.

I wanted to get past this little conversation, so I could go pick Anne-Marie up. There was no way I was leaving her. No way! She kept me sane and grounded. They didn't understand how much I needed her in my life or how much I wanted her to be a part of my life. Wherever you saw me, you saw Anne-Marie. We'd been an item for years.

"We're not asking you, son; we are telling you to break it off with her. You can wait until after graduation, but when you go to college I want you one hundred percent focused on school. We feel you won't be able to do that with Anne-Marie in the picture."

"We just love you so much, Damon. We want the best for you in life. You are not thinking about your future right now. We as your parents are looking out for your future and it's best if Anne-Marie not be any part of the brilliant future we know that you are going to have," mom said.

She had the nerve to look at me tenderly, as if that would make her words easier to accept. That moment went down in the record books.

It was the moment I lost all respect for my parents. All the respect I had for the great pastor and First Lady Gloria, evaporated at that moment. By asking me to reject the only girl I'd ever loved, they tore my heart from my chest and burned it to smithereens.

"Dad," I said with a plea in my voice. "You know how much I love Anne-Marie. I may only be eighteen, but I know I want to marry her. I want her to be the mother of my children." I said this with all the feelings of a grown man and not a child as my parents seemed to see me.

"Baby, trust me. You will get over that girl," my mother said with a sneer. "You will meet a nice Christian woman with high values that will come from a good Christian family. You can give us as many grandchildren as you want when that time comes. We will welcome it with open arms," she added.

"But…" I started to object, but was cut off by my father.

"Son, you may be angry now, but we have your best

interest at heart. You will thank us one of these days. You just wait and see," Dad said cutting me off. He thought he was reasoning with me, but really he was planting a seed of discontentment in our relationship. I didn't want that seed to be planted that day, but it was. I didn't want to ever water that seed, but if they really tried to force me to leave Anne-Marie, I didn't know what I would do.

"May I go now?" I asked.

"Of course you may go. Enjoy yourself tonight and remember absolutely no drinking and driving," Dad ordered.

"I know the drill," I said standing to leave.

My mother came over and adjusted my tie and collar. "I love you so much my handsome son," she said, grasping both sides of my face to pull down to place a kiss against my cheek. "You make us so proud!"

"I love you too, Mom," I said with a heavy heart. I thought my parents understood me. Even better, I thought I understood them before that night.

Of all nights, it was the night of my senior dance that they came at me with some bull like this. I thought about Anne-Marie's beautiful smile and the way she looked when she pouted over losing a game of Scrabble, or when she jumped into my arms with joy. I knew without a doubt I would never meet anyone like Anne-Marie. She was one of a kind. I smiled just at the thought of her.

I picked Anne-Marie up and we went to the dance. We danced to every slow song. I held her as close to me as I could. I inhaled her scent and took it into my memory. I listened to her heartbeat, remembering her rhythm. I ran my fingers over the grooves of her soft hand recalling every line. I kissed her lips tasting her tongue and enjoying the warmth of her beautiful mouth one last time, before I dropped her back off. From that night going forward, I knew nothing would ever be the same again. I made sure we enjoyed every moment we spent together up until graduation. Life without Anne-Marie would be no life at all…I was sure of it.

Over the next few weeks, my parents laid it on thick. They told me of all the things I would miss out on by binding myself with my high school sweetheart. They told me that there was so much more on the horizon. To toughen the deal, my mother even told me, "If you don't leave that girl alone, don't call here asking for anything!"

Even though I promised myself I would love Anne-Marie for the rest of my life, I respected my parents enough to extract my rib from my chest. I broke up with her right after we had spent the night celebrating graduation, by making love in the back seat of my Ford Explorer at Look-out Meadow. It hurt so bad to say goodbye, but I was convinced it was the best thing for both of us. We were headed in separate directions; me to college in another state and she had no concrete plans. One thing was for sure, I didn't think I would ever be able to purge Anne-Marie from my heart.

Chapter 1

Anne-Marie

I crossed my legs and uncrossed them as I sat in the first pew of Mount Hill Missionary Baptist Church. I squeezed my legs together as the strum of the organ music created a beat that sent electrical shocks that could be vivaciously felt in my pussy. I was pantiless and Pastor Damon Williams Jr. already knew it. He liked me that way. By the look on his face as he sat in the pastor's chair, he was remembering the night prior, just as I was. His brown eyes pierced into my soul as the choir gave their usual immaculate Sunday morning performance.

I wish that old biddy would hush up, I thought to myself as Sister Mary Beal's high-pitched voice wafted into my ears, hitting an off key high note. If she spent more time practicing her key than she did in other people's business, her old ass might've sounded worth a damn up there. That woman made my skin crawl. She loved to act as if her shit didn't stink, and then had the nerve to get up on that choir stand and praise God the loudest, until the next time she had somebody to whisper about.

At the close of what could have been a soul-stirring hymnal, Pastor Williams walked up to the podium in his two-button, black Brooks Brothers suit that was tailor made to perfection for his tall, muscular frame. I gave a secret smile, once I noticed the deep purple silk tie with white dots I had given him as a gift for his birthday.

He stood around six-four and wore a size twelve shoe. In the pastor's case, it was true what they said about men with big

138

feet. With ten inches of prime beef between his legs, he was definitely in the meat packing business. His wavy hair was cut low to his head and he was the color of coffee with extra cream mixed in. He was as near to perfection as they got. *Well, almost perfect,* I silently mused as my eyes slid over to the object of my contempt.

Nancy Williams, his pregnant wife, sat across the aisle from me on the first row, along with her mother-in-law, Gloria Williams, and the rest of the high society women in the church. Nancy was dressed befitting the first lady of the church. Her Elise jacket maternity dress showed off her high-rounded belly beneath her expensive dress. Her big hat sat atop her head to match her dress. She oozed sophistication and elegance. I was sure Nancy, the charming and sophisticated Christian woman, was just what Damon's parents ordered. A frown marred my brow as I thought back to my graduation night, May 28, 1999. That was the night that Damon saw fit to break my heart...

"I love you so much, Anne-Marie," Damon said as he thrust into me from the back seat of his Ford Explorer. His parents had given him the new truck as a graduation gift. My bare bottom was lying against the leather seat, dripping my pussy juices all over it.

"I love you too, Damon; I am just so glad that we can finally be together now," I panted as I grinded beneath his body with my legs wrapped around his waist.

Damon intensified his strokes as he vowed to love me forever. That night, as the moon beamed through the trees where we were parked at Look-out Meadows, I felt our love being cemented. I screamed my orgasm into the night as he pumped into me over and over again before joining me with an orgasm of his own.

He kissed me one last time before we put our clothes back on. He got out and waited for me to get out and get in the front seat, as he got behind the steering wheel. I fiddled with the radio and tuned into 95.5

FM. *Faith Evans voice crooned from the speakers singing "Never Gonna Let You Go." I turned towards him and song along with the lyrics before noticing the sad look in his eyes.*

"What is wrong, Damon?" I asked, becoming concerned by the deep sadness exuding from his brown eyes.

He took my hands in his, before kissing each hand tenderly. I smiled at him, but he didn't smile back. He just stared into my face as if he wanted to remember every detail of it. A tear suddenly fell down his left cheek before he quickly wiped it away on his shirt sleeve.

"You are scaring me, Damon. What is wrong?" I asked again as I touched his jawline tenderly.

"Promise me that you won't hate me, Anne-Marie."

"I could never hate you, Damon. You already know how much I love you, don't you?" I asked with a tender smile.

"I know…I love you so much too. I don't want to do this," he said taking a deep breath.

"Do what, Damon? What do you have to do?"

"I…I," he stuttered.

"Just say it, Damon," I said a bit impatiently.

He took another deep breath and exhaled. "I have to break up with you," he said sadly as tears slipped from his eyes.

I frowned, not believing his words. Did I just hear those words from the love of my life? I questioned myself silently. "What do you mean that you have to break up with me Damon? I know you have got to be joking," I said hoping against hope that he was.

"I am not joking. I am going away to college and it's just not going to work between us; I have to concentrate on my studies," he added as if trying to convince himself.

"Is this your idea or your parents, Damon? I already know they hate me…at least your mother does," I added a bit uncomfortably.

"It doesn't matter whose idea it was," he lied. "I just want you to know that I will always love you no matter what, Anne-Marie."

"I will wait for you, Damon," I said as hot tears burned behind my eyes and then leaked down my cheeks. "We can pretend you broke up with me and then we can still be together," I begged.

"No, it has to be this way, Anne-Marie. I can't lie to my parents…they would find out sooner than later. When it comes down to it, I can't disappoint them. They are sacrificing so much for me. I have to do as they asked," he said holding his head down as if he was too ashamed to look at me.

I saw there was no reasoning with him as my lips trembled from the tortured scream I held inside. "I hate you," I said with a pain-filled voice. "Take me home and I never want to see you again," I said even though I didn't mean a word of it from deep inside.

"Anne-Marie," he said.

I turned my head away from him and let my hair cover my face that held nothing but pain. "Take me home now," I shouted loudly, as I looked unseeingly out the truck's window into the darkness.

Damon started the vehicle without another word. Damon had broken my seventeen-year-old heart and I knew that nothing would ever be the same again…

I was drawn from that horrid memory and back to Damon's sexy baritone voice as he said, "I will be reading from the Song of Solomon today church. Those of you that have your bibles, turn to Solomon chapter seven, verses three through thirteen. And it reads," he said before looking into my eyes. Then, he looked around the church before stopping on his very pregnant wife. He gave her a wink and a smile before he continued reading. "Your breasts are like two fawns, twins of gazelle…"

My thoughts went to the night before as he continued reading the scripture. Damon had recited that verse to me just before he made love to me over and over again. I squirmed in my seat becoming lost in my salacious thoughts. I had no shame. It

141

didn't matter if I was in a crowded church surrounded by Christians and sinners like me. Thoughts of Damon and me doing the intimate tango came over me like a raging storm.

My pussy pulsated from the thought of Damon being wedged deep inside of me as I rode him cowgirl style. The strong grasp he had on my waist left red marks of his fingerprints, as I rode him hard and rode him well. His ten inches of hardness plunged in and out of my wet pussy. I coated his dick with sweet, sticky nectar. The harder he plunged into me the louder my moans became, as his name slipped from my lips again and again.

I knew my lusty thoughts had no place in church, but Damon had an effect on me. It didn't matter where I was; the baritone of his sexy voice sent chills down my body straight to the heated core between my thighs. I bit back a moan and squeezed my thighs together as Damon's deep voice penetrated through my lust hazed musings.

"You alright honey?" an older lady sitting beside me asked.

I reluctantly tore my eyes away from the pulpit. I could only answer with a nod of my head. I took the fan she offered to fan away the beads of perspiration on my upper lip. I fluttered the fan back and forth trying to cool myself down. The fan wasn't helping much at all, and I didn't expect it to. I knew the only thing that could help me was more of Damon between my thighs. The more that I had of him the more I wanted of him. I couldn't have him wholly the way I wanted to, so I looked forward to the stolen, passionate moments we shared.

After being busted by the older lady, I really tried my best to focus for the rest of the service. Thankfully, the order of service moved along in a timely fashion and it was not long before we all stood on one accord for benediction.

I breathed a sigh of relief as I stood in line with the rest of the congregation to greet the pastor and the deacons. My heart beat rapidly as I got closer to Damon. My excitement for Damon Williams would never wane. I was still that giddy schoolgirl who fell head over heels in love with him, even after he hurt me the way he did. I pushed that thought away quickly. The past was the past, at least that's what I told myself. Our relationship was not perfect, but we were back together and we were definitely building something special.

"Hello Sister Anne-Marie. It is *so* good to see you in attendance on this fine Sunday," Pastor Williams said when it was time for me to greet him. He hugged me as he did all of his members.

"Why thank you, Pastor," I said leaning into his embrace. Damon's cologne immediately assailed my nostrils. "I'm not wearing any panties," I whispered softly in his ear. "I wouldn't have missed today's service for anything in the world and your message was on point," I said in a louder voice.

"Thanks, Sister Anne-Marie. I do try."

"Oh, and I have always loved having the Song of Solomon recited to me," I said as I pulled back to briefly look into his eyes. He gave my hand an extra squeeze.

"Thank you, sister, I aim to please," he said with double meaning.

I had to take a step back, before I thrust my tongue down his throat right there in the sanctuary for the whole congregation to see, including his wife. I bit back a moan. His blatant display of masculinity called to me. He finally released my hand and I proceeded down the line, only glancing over my shoulder once at his six-feet-four inches of fineness.

I was greeted by more members on my way out the door. I smiled and nodded politely. I didn't have time to stand around and chit chat all day with those nosy ass biddies, who portrayed a holier than thou attitude. Sister Mary Beal's non-singing tail was one of the old biddies I was speaking of and I saw her heading my way.

Sister Mary knew and told more gossip than the Herald and Times put together. I could hear her same questions now. *Anne-Marie why aren't you married with two or three kids by now? When this and when that?* I walked quickly to my car and unlocked the door, with a press to my key chain. I was in the car and backing out my parking spot before Sister Mary made it halfway to my car. I threw a wave her way as I drove away from the church to get on the freeway, heading towards my two-bedroom apartment located in Lincoln Park.

*

I inserted the key to open my apartment door and stepped inside. I closed the door and kicked off my Stuart Weitzman stilettos. I wiggled my toes in relief before burying them down in the thick, fluffy carpet of my living room floor. My phone vibrated from my handbag and I reached inside to retrieve it. It was a text message from Damon.

"Babe, you looked good enough to eat today. Stop tempting me with that pretty pussy during my sermon or I will make you pay. See you later, so be ready."

I smiled as I put the phone down on my coffee table and sat on the sofa. I lay back on the sofa cushions as a tingle began in my pussy at the thought of seeing Damon again. I have loved that man since forever it seemed. In actuality, it had been since tenth grade. We were together for three whole years, until our graduation date. Just when I thought our dreams were beginning, they were shattered in the blink of an eye.

"Damn…" The hurtful past just kept rearing its ugly head, no matter how much I tried to keep it at bay. I thought about Pastor Williams Sr. and his wife Gloria Williams. His mom and dad had other ideas for Damon and those ideas didn't include me in any shape or form. His upper-class parents didn't think I was good enough for their only son. I was a loose girl with no morals. I was raised in a single-parent home with no father in sight.

I was sure his mother was the ring leader. I never understood why I wasn't good enough for her. I never treated her unkindly, even if she looked down her snooty, superficial Christian, or so-called Christian nose at me.

Damon went far away to college and fulfilled his parents'

wishes. He was the good son, who eventually followed in his father footsteps by taking over as pastor when Damon Sr. retired. He even gave up his position as an Engineer in the business world to satisfy his father in becoming a full-time pastor of Mt. Hill Missionary Baptist Church. He was also the son that married the proper and elegant Nancy Gates, just like his parents wanted. She was everything his parents wanted in a daughter-in-law. She came from the perfect Christian up-to-do family with money and prestige. She became Mrs. Damon Williams…a preacher's wife who was loved and adored by the entire congregation, except me. His parents were expecting their first grandchild and they were all beyond ecstatic.

She may have worn the ring and even had the marriage license saying that Damon was her husband. She may even be having his child, but I knew deep down that I had the most important thing of all. I had his heart and he had mine. Damon promised to love me forever and his wife wasn't going to stop me from claiming what should have belonged to me a long time ago, and neither were his parents.

Visit www.nayberrypublications.com to purchase your next page turning read.

CPSIA information can be obtained at www.ICGtesting.com
Printed in the USA
LVOW10s1729071016

507864LV00014B/660/P

9 781943 179299